Wishes Under a Highland Star

by

Mary Morgan

A Tale from the Order of the Dragon Knights

Wishes Under a Highland Star

The Wild Rose Press, Inc.
PO Box 708
Adams Basin, NY 14410-0708
Visit us at www.thewildrosepress.com

Publishing History
First Edition, 2022
Trade Paperback ISBN 978-1-5092-4435-5
Digital ISBN 978-1-5092-4436-2

A Tale from the Order of the Dragon Knights
Published in the United States of America

Her stubborn refusal to leave intrigued Alex. Would she flee if he challenged her? He lowered his head near hers. "Why do ye care?"

Her eyes widened, and her luscious lips parted. "Because I do," she whispered.

Alex's breathing became shallow and the air around them thick. Her pink lips begged to be kissed. Would they be as sweet as berries? Or as heady as the wine he drank last evening? An ache to take her in his arms filled him.

He wrestled with the conflict—duty, honor, possession. She was pure as new-fallen snow on a crisp morn, and he no better than a rutting stag. Though his hands shook to hold her in his arms, Alex steeled his emotions and moved away from her.

Ye deserve a better man, Aine. Ye are a beauty, and I am but a beast.

Aine's smile came slowly as she took a step toward him and did the unthinkable. Standing on her tiptoes, she brushed a kiss along his bearded cheek. "Is it wrong to care for ye?"

Indecision plagued him as he regarded her—disbelieving, curious as to what his real fear might be. Shoving aside the conflict within, Alex grasped her around the waist. He nuzzled the spot below her ear. "Ye tempt your fate with a kiss, Aine? With a man ye do not ken?"

She lifted her gaze to his—her cheeks flushed with a rosy hue. "Did I tempt ye?"

Praise for Mary Morgan

"I recommend not only '*Rorik*' but also the previous book '*Magnar*' too! A great series well written with intrigue, love, and fantasy."

~*Nicole Laverdure for Books and Benches*
~*~

"A beautifully written Viking paranormal romance, *Rorik* is a must-read this summer. Highly recommend!"

~ *N.N. Light's Book Heaven*
~*~

"Dark suspense and sexual tension ripple across these pages from the very first chapter. Mary Morgan brings ancient Scotland to life in vivid and pulse-pounding detail. It's brilliantly and masterfully done."

~ *InD'tale Magazine July/August 2021 Issue*
~*~

"This is not just a book about romance, but a journey of emotions that will make you laugh, cry, and want more."

~ *Mistress of Book Reviews*
~*~

"I will just say this book was riveting from start to finish and I devoured it!"

~ *Jan Sikes for Writing and Music*

Dedication

For John.
I made a wish, and you took a chance. Thank you for
believing in fairy tales and our love.

Prologue

Secrets.

The Fae have many secrets tucked beneath their realm. Far below the shimmering layers of magic hide the darker, unspoken deeds—where the Fae men ascended from their realm and took human females. They craved to taste the forbidden flesh of a mortal.

Often, when the Fae became disillusioned during their time in the earthly world, they vanished through the veil and returned to their home. However, a cruel fate awaited those who lingered far too long. The icy fingers of death claimed those Fae who remained in the world of mortals.

And what they left behind were the innocent. Children who were born from these unions—*children* who were part *Fae* and *human*.

Countless human women died in childbirth, leaving bairns abandoned and left to forge their own destiny with other families. The Fae refused to acknowledge them. Or mayhap they were unaware of the magnitude of what had transpired with the birth of these children.

In the beginning, there were merely a few children. But as the centuries passed within the Fae's glittering realm, their numbers increased.

Soon, whispers floated on rose-scented breezes to the crystal palace of the Fae, specifically to the Fae King and Queen.

These half-Fae could no longer be denied.

Furious over this revelation, the Fae King's anger burned fierce in his proclamation. An edict was swiftly issued, and a Guardian appointed to protect, defend, and guide these *misfit* children on their true path within the human world. Until they were ready to venture forth on their own as adults, they would remain cloaked in secret within the mists of Scotland and Ireland.

Rarely did anyone see within this veiled, magical haven. The shields woven incredibly strong by the Fae King.

Yet for one Scottish chieftain on a quest, he uncovered the truth one snowy night when a half-Fae lass made not one, but *many* wishes under a Highland star.

Chapter One

Leòmhann Castle ~ Early December 1210

"Did they really fly across the mountains, Lady Gwen?" asked the young lass, her eyes alight and eager to hear more.

"Aye. I would never spout a falsehood."

Murmured voices from the other children echoed around the lady.

"Let her finish the story, and then ye can ask your questions," ordered one of the older lads.

She smiled in approval at him. "'Tis almost near the end."

Alex MacFhearguis listened in rapt attention to the story unfolding within the great hall. The woman had a musical lilt to her tone, even as she shifted the bairn in her arms. The tale was most certainly folly—a tale woven from fantasy. Yet he found himself unable to walk away. Though she possessed great skills as a weaver of tapestries, he pondered if she was also gifted as a bard.

While he leaned against the stone wall, a smile twitched at the corners of his mouth. If the children had been older, would they find this purely trifle like he did? He yearned to add his question to the countless others but refrained.

Patrick approached and nudged him. "She weaves a

powerful tale, aye?"

Arching a brow in disbelief at his brother's words, he disputed, "She speaks of *deer* flying, and a giant elf dressed in a red cloak who guides these deer. And their home is in the far north covered in ice and *sugar*."

"Aye, *aye*. 'Tis a strange story—one I have heard her tell our son." Patrick brushed a hand down the back of his neck.

Alex snorted in disbelief. "Are ye certain your wife is not one of the Fae?"

Mirth danced in his brother's eyes. "I can assure ye my wife is *not* a Fae. Simply a woman who tumbled back in time when she pulled on a cursed thread around our giant yew tree."

Returning his gaze to the scene near the blazing hearth, Alex asked softly, "Did ye ask the elder weavers to strip the remaining thread?"

Patrick chuckled. "Aye, with the help of Gwen. They even blessed the tree. The curse is broken and buried."

Alex shuddered. "Good. I have nae desire to have any other women from another time venturing onto our land."

"Fearing one will come for ye?" chided Patrick.

Alex glared at his brother. "None will be welcomed."

His harsh response did not discourage his brother. The man clucked his tongue in disapproval. "'Tis a wonder any woman would talk to ye with the fierce looks ye gave to those we greeted this summer."

"Did I invite them to Leòmhann? Nae." Alex recoiled at the memory.

"They traveled with their fathers, who ye

summoned."

"To discuss the terms within the Great Glen, *not* marriage contracts," corrected Alex, scratching at several days' growth of beard.

"If I recall, I warned ye this would happen when the first man arrived with his daughter following swiftly behind him."

Alex muttered a curse. "Do not remind me. It was a wretched summer of escaping boring conversations and tense discussions over the ongoing threat of King John within our lands."

Patrick lowered his voice. "Ye forgot your manners on more than one occasion, and ye ken I was not speaking about your talks with the other chieftains."

"'Tis always good to ken ye were nearby to remind me of my duties," Alex responded dryly.

"I fear ye frightened many a young lass. Your sullen demeanor did not go well with some of their fathers." Patrick tapped a finger to his chin. "I believe ye reduced the Campbell lass to a fit of tears after she presented ye with a gift."

Crossing his arms over his chest, Alex fought the urge to wipe the smirk from his brother's face with his fist. "Can ye not imagine my shock to find she had made me a cap to wear at night while sleeping?"

Patrick coughed into his fist. "Ye did not need to tell the lass that ye prefer to sleep *without* any clothing."

Shrugging, Alex responded, "'Tis the truth. At least she took the item with her when she fled my solar."

"By the Gods, ye are a boar's ass. And ye, our *chieftain*."

Alex narrowed his eyes. "Ye cannot tell me ye would not have done the same."

"I would have taken a gentler approach."

Laughter bellowed forth from Alex, releasing the tension within his bones. Quickly recovering, he explained, "By *gentler*, ye would have rather bedded them and then risk the wrath of their fathers. I chose to be honest."

"Might I remind ye I am now married. *Happily* married," protested Patrick.

"I was speaking of your former self—before ye met Gwen!"

The children twisted toward them with looks of censure, and the babe in Gwen's arms let out a wail of protest.

Alex raised his hand outward. "Forgive my outburst. Do continue."

Ignoring both men, the woman soothed her son with quiet words and kisses while the children waited patiently for her.

Silence reigned between Alex and his brother, leaving Gwen to resume her tale.

Patrick exhaled softly. "'Tis a scene I never tire witnessing."

He didn't need to ask what scene. Patrick's love for his wife changed and consumed his brother. And why Patrick felt the need to continually discuss a wife for him only stirred Alex's ire further. Aye, he did consider reaching out beyond the Great Glen for a wife, but he tossed the idea to the winds numerous moons ago. Known for his harsh words and outbursts, Alex left many lasses in tears or worse, they fled in fear of him. He simply did not possess the qualities of speaking to women.

And to have one woman control him frightened

Alex.

He'd witnessed what happened with his brothers. Patrick had found his woman, and Adam as well.

An ache surfaced whenever his thoughts drifted to their younger brother. He had fought in the Crusades and returned unharmed. However, no one could have prepared them for the reality that Adam MacFhearguis was destined for something more. To become a Dragon Knight and live out the remainder of his life in the future with his beloved.

He rubbed the heel of his palm over his heart as if to ease the loss. *May ye be well, Adam. May ye live long. May ye have many sons.*

This silent prayer sent out into the mists each morn and night. Alex never failed in his message, praying his brother would somehow hear his words.

His gaze returned to Patrick. "Ye have been blessed," he murmured.

"With Gwen, aye," he acknowledged. "But to hold my son—*David*—within my arms is a feeling I cannot explain." Turning toward his brother, Patrick continued, "Until ye make the first step, ye cannot understand, Alex. Did we not have this discussion several moons ago?"

Alex dismissed him with a wave of his hand, growing weary of the same conversation. "Perchance Leòmhann is meant for ye and your sons."

Patrick's brow creased. "Nae, not true. Do not speak thus."

"Why not?" challenged Alex. "Michael was the eldest until his early demise. Did ye not consider this may be your and Gwen's destiny?"

"Ye are tired, Brother."

"Aye. Weary of discussing my fate about marriage,"

protested Alex.

His brother wrapped an arm around his shoulder. "Let us make a wager on this day, aye?"

Alex gave him a skeptical glance, unsure if he should remain a second longer in the great hall. "Ye always did enjoy a challenge."

"And ye didn't?"

Stepping free from his brother's embrace, Alex's gaze bore into him. "Do not keep me waiting."

Patrick placed a hand over his chest. "Ye wound me. I have never—"

"I can count the numerous times ye have kept us all waiting at Leòmhann, *Brother*. Now, state your wager before I take my leave."

Striding toward one of the tables, Patrick picked up a jug of ale and filled two cups. Returning to Alex's side, he handed one outward. "Since the snows have descended, your search for a wife must be delayed, aye?"

Alex took the offered drink. "*Aye*," he responded hesitantly.

"I shall give ye the winter months to consider those who have stirred a passable interest in ye—"

"There have been none," Alex interrupted and then drank deeply from his cup.

Patrick ignored him. "When the snows thaw come early spring, if ye have not made a decision, I shall make the choice for ye and invite them here. I ken there were a couple who caught your interest."

Sputtering on his ale, Alex wiped his mouth with the back of his hand. "'Tis not for ye to find me a *wife*. This conversation is finished."

After taking a sip from his cup, Patrick shrugged. "Are ye fearing ye would lose the wager? I never knew ye as a man who would refuse a challenge."

"We are talking about my life," he hissed out.

"Wife," corrected Patrick.

"By the hounds, ye ken they are the same."

Alex stormed to the table and refilled his cup. *For all I ken ye would choose one with a face of a goat and who would talk unceasingly.* A dull ache settled behind his eyes, and he rubbed a hand over his brow. If he did not end this wretched conversation, Alex feared his brother would dwell on this argument all winter.

Walking to his side, Patrick leaned against the table.

Alex glared at him. An inspiration grew within his thoughts. "I accept your challenge. Though if I should find a suitable woman to become my wife *before* the snow thaws, ye must pay my wager."

Patrick's eyes widened in surprise. "Ye want coin?"

Alex chuckled softly while shaking his head. "Nae, nae. I will give ye *my* terms upon my victory. Ye did mention this is a wager, aye?"

Patrick groaned. "I do not ken if I should be overjoyed at the prospect of ye considering my wager *or* if I should be worried what awaits me if ye win."

Poking a finger into his brother's chest, Alex smiled fully. "Ye should be careful when ye interfere with another man's life. Now, what plans have ye and Alastair MacKay made for the midwinter feast? Will he provide us with mead in exchange for venison and boar meat? I hope ye mentioned the trade with him during your recent time at Aonach Castle."

After grumbling a curse, Patrick placed his cup onto the table.

"By the hounds, ye forgot." Alex drained the rest of his cup and licked his lips. "Nae wine and little ale will not set well with the others we provide for here."

"The MacKay clan will journey the week before midwinter and stay for a month," blurted out Patrick.

Stunned, Alex took a few steps back. "Lugh's balls! The entire clan? Here at *Leòmhann*?"

Patrick nodded slowly, wariness reflecting within his eyes.

Alex pinched the bridge of his nose in frustration. "Do ye ken how many *Dragon Knights* will be under our roof? Along with their wives and children?"

"They are friends—"

Dismissing his brother with a wave of his hand, he argued, "Aye, they are nae longer our enemy, but ye do realize the power they can wield? Suppose there is an argument? They could rain down the might of fire, storms, water, *or* the ground opening beneath our feet and burying us."

"Seriously, Alex? Why are ye being stubborn?"

Avoiding Patrick's censure, he demanded, "Whose bloody idea was it to invite them here?"

Soft laughter came forth from Gwen. "The plan is *mine*."

Alex snapped his attention to the woman in disbelief. This is why he would never take a wife. *She would betray me.* "There is nae humor in this news."

"Surely ye can understand this is our first winter feast since our marriage," pleaded Patrick. In a gentler tone, he added, "Gwen truly wished to welcome the MacKays into our home. She has spoken with the other wives, and they have been in agreement."

Glancing sideways at his brother, he asked, "The last time she spoke with the MacKay women was late spring. Are ye telling me they"—he waved a hand outward—"have planned this for months?"

"In truth, Bridget thought of the idea," confessed Gwen.

"The MacKay women can be verra convincing," argued Patrick, stepping in front of him.

Alex wanted to fling his cup against the wall. "'Tis an outrage that not one person consulted me—their chieftain with this plan."

"We had a bountiful harvest, and Alastair will provide the mead. They are also providing the meat from a recent hunt," explained Patrick, removing the cup from Alex's hand.

Fighting to keep his anger contained, he asked, "Again, why must they all gather here? Cannot a quiet feast be enough?"

"Would ye like more ale, now that ye ken there will be mead in a few weeks?"

Alex crossed his arms over his chest. "Ye have not answered my questions."

Shrugging, Patrick announced, "More ale for me."

"If ye are to persist with this argument, please do so out of the hall. I'm attempting to finish my tale," ordered Gwen.

The children all nodded or grumbled their acknowledgement at Gwen's pronouncement.

Alex could offer no harsh retort. His fury so great, the words he wanted to fling out became lodged like a stale bannock within his throat.

The woman obviously deemed she was the new chieftain of Leòmhann Castle.

This is exactly why I shall never marry. Women, specifically wives, twist your words to their will. What I require is a long ride into the hills to rid this uneasiness and conversation.

"I require some fresh air," he grumbled.

Unfolding his arms, Alex stormed out of the hall, determined to get far away from any more talk of feasting, Dragon Knights, *and* women.

Chapter Two

"Remember, there are always two veils within the starlight." ~Fae Lore

"Do ye trust me?" whispered Aine, treading carefully across the moss-laden path between the pines. Dead leaves and twigs crunched under her booted feet as she peered ahead at her destination. Moonlight dusted the path in front of them, giving her hope they were drawing near.

The wolfhound padded around in front of her and slipped away under a heaving branch.

"'Tis not the way I wish to travel," she bit out into the chilled night air.

Halting her steps, Aine drew her cloak more firmly over her head. She dared not shout at the animal for fear the dog would wander on without her. *I should not have brought ye with me.*

She knelt on one knee and pounded the moist ground with her fist. Waiting a few more heartbeats, Aine grew impatient.

When the dog refused to emerge, she blew the words outward. "Return to me, Etain. I will not ask ye again," she warned.

An owl hooted from above her. Aine grimaced at the intruder and slowly rose to standing. "Are ye saying I should do her bidding, Mab? Does she seek the same place as I?"

Dark eyes shone back at her as she glanced upward. Aine shook her head. "Give me an answer, Mab, or I shall go forth alone."

When the owl remained silent, Aine tapped her foot in annoyance.

"Perchance I am the fool?" Quickly realizing her mistake, she held out her hand. "Nae, do not answer that question."

The owl ruffled its feathers and turned away from her.

Resigned, Aine uttered a curse and followed after the wolfhound.

Tree limbs smacked at her along the way, their sting mocking her attempt toward her goal. Twice, Aine slipped, and twice she reminded herself she should have ventured forward on the other path. Though the moon's light was a beacon on this misty night, she feared the animal was leading her back to the protection of warm shelter and comforts of its bed.

"Never again will I bring ye on a journey at night, Etain. Are your bones too weary for the adventure? I did warn ye the night's icy fingers would creep through your thick fur. But nae, ye chose to come with me."

Aine's breath billowed white puffs around her as she trudged on through the dense trees and an unfamiliar path.

Slipping on a patch of mud, she quickly grasped the nearest branch to right herself. "There shall be nae kind words when I set my eyes on ye, beast."

She wiped her bruised hand down her cloak and cast a furtive glance upward. As the mists parted, the stars hung heavy against the black night. Yet something appeared wrong. Frowning, Aine took in the other stars. "'Tis as if the Gods and Goddesses shook out their brilliance and reordered them," she murmured.

Etain gave a low yapping sound, alerting her to the animal's presence.

"Finally." Making haste, she moved steadily after the animal.

When she passed the last tree, the area opened up, revealing a glorious view. Her gaze traveled along the length of the stream while the soothing water rippled over large moss-covered boulders. Her past visits in the great forest were always shrouded with numerous trees making the stream appear smaller. Aine pressed a fist to her chest. The moon shimmered over the water like jewels. Never had she been in this area of the great forest, and she found herself rooted to the spot.

She spread her arms wide. "'Tis a scene I shall never forget."

The wolfhound lumbered to Aine's side.

"Why are ye showing me this place now? And here I was spouting harsh words at ye." A nervous laugh escaped from Aine as she placed a gentle hand on her companion's head. "Forgive me, old friend? Ye ken how quick my temper can fire, aye?"

The wolfhound raised its head and licked her fingers.

Aine let out a sigh of relief. "Then all is forgiven. I thank ye."

Returning her gaze outward, she continued to take in the beauty while the stream wove its own music—the sound dancing over smooth rocks and fallen tree trunks. Snow drifted in lazy wisps, dusting the ground with their magic. How many nights had she made this journey under a full moon? *Too many moons.*

"Is this the time to make another wish? Have ye led me here for a reason?"

Etain let out a yawn and stretched her legs forward. With a sigh, she then settled back on her hind legs.

"Ye are silent this night. Yet ye ken what must be done, and I grow weary of waiting."

Withdrawing the small blade from the leather belt at her waist, Aine brushed her fingers over the cold steel. Holding the blade outward, she marveled at her craftmanship. The small *sgian dubh* took weeks to forge by her hand. She rubbed her thumb over the crystal fashioned within the hilt of the small blade and smiled.

"Would ye be proud of me, Father?" she uttered softly, recalling his hands guiding hers within the forge years ago. A tear trickled down her cheek, and Aine swiftly brushed away the annoying moisture, along with her folly emotions. She'd watched her father become weak after her mother left them, and then he descended into melancholy toward the end of his days. His grief left him with no strength to care for her and her brother. And her mother was nae better, abandoning them so many years ago.

Yet whenever Aine fashioned anything from the smithy, or created a carving from a fallen tree, she yearned to show her work to him.

"Why did ye have to die so young, Father?" Her anguish tormented and frustrated her.

But her fury at her mother grew with each passing year.

"Ye are a vile person to forsake us." Aine spat on the ground and lowered her arm, trying to quell the burning anger.

She swallowed the hateful words she ached to spit out. *'Tis not the time to dwell on the past.* Aine firmly believed her mother would be dealt her punishment from the Goddess. She bit her lower lip, squashing the rest of her turmoil, and took a step forward.

"If my heart speaks truthfully, then my wish will be granted."

She swept a glance at Etain. "Do ye not agree? Do ye not yearn to see beyond to other villages in Scotland? Or to have a traveler enter our realm, and we can journey out of here with them? Do ye not grow weary of the wait?"

The wolfhound regarded her for several heartbeats but resumed her gaze outward.

Pushing back the hood of her cloak, Aine stepped forward. Once again, she lifted the blade to the moon glow. The light bounced off the crystal in an array of tiny jewels. Now was the moment to speak her words.

She drew in a deep breath and released the air slowly on the exhale.

"From the east, the rising sun, I welcome ye. From the south, where the fire burns bright, I welcome ye. From the North, where we call our home, I welcome ye. From the west, the land of forever, I welcome ye. And from the stars, great guardians who watch over us, I welcome ye."

Leaves swirled in a dance around her feet, and she drew in the power of the ancients with each indrawn breath.

Bending down on one knee, Aine traced a symbol in the dirt and leaves. As she rose, she did the same within the chilled air. "Hear my plea, Guardians. I, daughter of human and Fae, beseech ye to hear my call. Grant me the power to bend the veils between the realms. Let another see beyond and into our world. Allow them to enter, for now is the time."

Aine waved the blade in the air and then bent and tapped the ground. "As above so 'tis within."

Her hands shook as she lifted them outward. Did her request push her words beyond to be woven with magic? A small voice whispered inside her mind to stop this at once. However, when the stars drifted closer to Aine, she shoved aside her doubts and raised her voice. Her words carried across the landscape, repeating her plea in an echo. With one final slash in the air with her blade, she blew out her words. "Let the one who ye judge worthy, enter."

"What have ye done, Aine Fraser!" Her uncle's voice bellowed behind her.

The void around her snapped with a resounding clap of thunder, sending her slamming against a tree. As she fought for air, Aine dropped her *sgian dubh* to the ground. A great humming filled her head, and she placed her fingers to her temple. Doing her best to rid the last remnants of pain, she tried to steady her breathing.

Etain rose and barked at the intruder.

"Silence!" ordered the man.

Yet the wolfhound would not be deterred and moved to Aine's side.

Aine lifted her head to meet her uncle's harsh glare.

"I will not ask ye again." His stance was one she had never witnessed. He kept his hands fisted by his sides while his eyes flashed silver.

Aine never feared her uncle. Until this moment.

She swallowed. "I made another wish."

Her uncle slashed the air with his hand. "Nae! Ye

did more this time!"

Confusion marred her thinking. "I do…not understand."

"A wish is a simple request under the stars," he snapped, pointing a warning finger at the wolfhound when she uttered a low growl.

Frowning, Aine argued, "But that is what I did, Uncle Eamon."

"By the hounds of Cúchulainn! Ye ken there was more to the words ye spouted. Ye drew the power within ye and used magic."

Aine's heart beat rapidly against her chest. Was her uncle correct? Did she violate a vow she took years ago not to use magic in this village? She clenched her hands by her sides, recalling how the power surged inside her. Never before had she felt her body so alive with the elements and the ancients. She believed her request purely made from her heart, spoken to the Guardians of the stars.

Unsure of how to respond to her uncle, she lifted her head to the stars. Their previous splendor now shadowed by the mists drifting by. And within her soul she knew the answer.

Resuming her attention to her uncle, she clasped her hands together. "My apologies for the grave mishap."

"*Why*?" he demanded harshly.

"I grew weary waiting for a traveler," she responded truthfully. "The more I spoke, the more the words flowed from me."

Raking a hand through his hair, he paced in front of her. Ancient words poured forth from him—ones she understood well since her father had used them toward the end of his life in his lessons with her.

Uncle Eamon halted his steps and studied her. "Ye are one of the oldest here, my Aine," he stated in a gentler tone, adding, "Ye ken the edicts more than the others. Ye are not allowed to use magic to call forth someone beyond the veil. Only when I and the elders judge ye are ready. Then *I* shall wield the magic to either call someone to ye or send ye out into their world. Can ye honestly say ye had nae knowledge of what ye were doing?"

Her shoulders slumped. She had failed again. This was why Aine was not ready to venture outside the village. To do so would bring harm to the others, specifically her brother. Did they not all depend on her to lead a life without magic? And what if she left with the traveler and something happened to her beyond her village? If she dared to use her magic, death might be her punishment, and her brother would be doomed to face another loss.

Aine's heart ached. As always, her lack of patience proved to be her greatest failing.

"Perchance I am not meant to go beyond the veil, Uncle."

His brow furrowed, and he stepped toward her. "Is this what ye truly want?" He cupped her chin. "To stay forever inside this haven? Even Keegan understands that one day ye will go forth and make a life outside of here in Scotland."

She snorted. "My brother's reasons are selfish. He does not want his younger sister keeping watch on his antics. I believe he's been making his own wishes."

When her uncle dropped his hand, his mouth twitched with humor. "Aye, but not the ones ye have been making under a moonlit night in a *sacred* area."

Aine gasped and then narrowed her eyes at the wolfhound.

Uncle Eamon gave a low whistle. "So Etain led ye here?"

"Ye could have prepared me," she mumbled to the animal.

Her uncle rubbed a hand over his chin in thought. "Would ye have listened to her counsel?"

Heat infused Aine's cheeks. When did she ever consider another's advice unless they mirrored her own? Even when the animals spoke to her, Aine often disregarded their wisdom.

Uncle Eamon placed a firm hand on her shoulder. "I must consult the elders to seek a way of keeping the veil sealed. Give your apologies to the ancients and the Guardians in the night sky. Then return to your home. A storm is brewing. If Keegan finds ye have slipped out into the night again, he will have harsh words for ye."

Giving her uncle a curt nod, Aine bent and retrieved her *sgian dubh*. Placing the blade securely within the belt at her waist, she watched him depart and then glanced over her shoulder.

"Stop hiding in the shadows. I ken ye have been listening to our conversation."

"Ye should have told him the truth," scolded her brother, emerging from the other side of the trees.

Aine brushed out the leaves and pine needles from her cloak. "What truth, Keegan?"

"'Tis not your first time wielding the magic."

She lifted her gaze to meet his scorn. Aine would not cower in front of her brother. "And ye do not?"

Keegan's features turned to fury. "Ye ken nothing!" Tossing away one last leaf off her cloak, she regarded him with disdain. "Nothing? I ken where ye go after ye have finished your chores. Ye are nae better." She waved her hand about. "Ye desire to leave and journey to the other side just as much as I do."

Her brother fisted his hands on his hips. "I do not use magic, Aine!"

Etain lumbered between them.

"'Tis not what I have heard," she argued, ruffling her fingers through Etain's coarse hair.

Glancing sharply at the wolfhound, Keegan's eyes grew wide. "Traitor animal."

Laughter bubbled up within Aine, spilling forth. The look on her brother's face was one she'd never forget. Her secret now revealed to him.

"I suppose *all* the animals report to ye, aye?" he spouted with disgust.

She arched a brow. "Not all. There are some who remain loyal to ye."

Keegan kicked aside a stone. "If ye must ken, I choose to learn about magic within our realm and only with guidance from one of the elders. I have and will not *ever* use the power to part the veil."

Curious, she asked, "So ye think my wishes turned to *magic*?"

Her brother shrugged. "The stars did shine brightly for a brief moment, and I felt as if I stood between two realms."

"Why did ye follow me?" Aine asked, linking her arm through his.

"When ye left our home, I became worried. Then Mab guided me to ye."

"There is nae need to fret, Keegan," she soothed. "Unless ye sensed a foreboding of looming danger?"

He clasped her hand within the crook of his arm. "Hard to determine, but—"

Footsteps approaching halted their conversation, and Keegan placed a finger against her lips.

Noting the confusion on her features, he bent his head near her ear. "Not Uncle Eamon. Remain here."

Keegan touched the animal's head and unsheathed his sword. Silently, he slipped into the trees.

Etain's growl rumbled low as she moved to a protective stance in front of Aine.

While Aine's hand clutched the blade at her belt, a cold breeze lifted a few strands of hair across her face. She fought to keep her breathing steady.

The minutes drifted by in agonizing torture while she waited for the intruder or Keegan to return. She tapped her foot in irritation and bit her tongue to keep silent. Aine strained to pick up any movement from her brother or another.

A shadow loomed within two trees, and slowly a man stepped forth. Uncertainty marred his features. He kept his hand secured over the hilt of his sword, and Aine felt trapped within his dark gaze as he continued to study her. Her mind unable to form any words while she stared at the giant intruder.

Should she greet him, flee, or scream? Even Etain appeared in awe of the man and kept silent.

Where are ye, Keegan?

The man took a step forward, entering the moonlight. "Why are ye here? Alone?"

The burr of his voice swept over her. Aine drew in a sharp breath but not from fear. This was no ordinary man. Nae. He was magnificent. A true warrior carved from the Gods. Never before had she seen another man like this one. He left her unsteady, weak, and she craved to know more.

She lifted her chin and smiled fully. "What are ye called?"

Too late to stop him, Aine watched in stunned horror as Keegan slipped silently behind her warrior and bashed him over the head with the hilt of his sword.

Chapter Three

"Wisdom of the heart is far more powerful than all the knowledge in the Library of the Ancients." ~Fae Lore

"Great Goddess! What have ye done?" Aine dropped to the ground beside the wounded man.

"Saving ye from this wretched creature," her brother spat out.

Her hands shook as she inspected the man's injury to the back of his head. "Ye are foolish, Keegan. He is simply a man."

Pointing a warning finger at her, he argued, "Nae. He is a *man* who could have brought harm to ye. This is your doing. Ye called him here when ye split the veil without permission."

Grumbling a curse, Aine ignored her brother's scolding and continued to inspect the damage. Blood oozed forth from the jagged wound. "Bring me some moss," she ordered.

Keegan snarled at her. "I will not help ye. Leave him. We must alert Uncle Eamon and the elders."

I do not take orders from ye. Swiftly rising, Aine shoved past her brother and went to collect some fresh moss.

When she returned, Keegan grabbed her arm. "We cannot tend to him. Let him return to his land."

Her laugh cold and bitter. "He is now in our realm—

our land. To leave him in the cruel weather is not wise. Snow is falling heavily."

Her brother shook his head but refrained from speaking.

She glared at him. "We shall tend to his wound at our home—a wound ye inflicted on him. When the man has recovered and wakes, I shall lead him back through the veil."

"*We?*" he echoed in their dense surroundings.

Aine knelt beside the man and resumed her task by applying the moss to his wound. "Aye. Did ye think I was speaking to Etain?" She dared not risk looking at her brother and kept to her task.

"And your plans to transport him back to our home?" he demanded harshly.

Smiling with the knowledge, she replied, "Call forth one of the horses from the village. I am certain Mab is nearby and ye can send her to deliver the message, even though it will take time for the horse to reach us. With the two of us, we can lift him onto the animal."

Keegan kicked a booted foot against the man's leg. "His weight is more than the cairn of stones on the hill."

Ignoring her brother, Aine withdrew her *sgian dubh* and slashed through her gown. Taking the strip of material, she fashioned the piece around the man's head, making sure the moss remained firmly secured. She brushed away the snow from his chiseled features and strong jaw. After wiping a hand over her brow, Aine brushed her fingers across his temples to ease any pain within.

Swiftly returning the small blade inside her belt, Aine deemed she had done all she could. Once at their dwelling, she'd offer up prayers for more healing.

Keegan hissed out another curse. "Did ye just give him some of your magic?"

"Have ye called for a horse?" she insisted, dismissing his disapproval of her healing qualities.

Her brother snapped his fingers, and one of their horses trotted forward.

Rising slowly, Aine arched her brow. "Your magic is growing, Brother."

"While ye have used yours for wishes, I have gained the wisdom of my magic if I make the decision to remain here."

Stunned by his declaration, Aine yearned to ask more questions. She'd thought his purpose was to seek beyond their home into Scotland—to make a life among the other humans without using magic. Never did he mention this new direction for his life. Why would he want to remain here?

An icy snowflake trickled down her cheek, and she shivered. *Another time for this discussion, Brother.* She shoved aside the conflict within her. They needed to get the man to shelter.

"Time to leave," she murmured, touching a gentle hand over the horse's mane. "Can ye lower yourself to aid us, Drust?"

The horse whinnied softly, and then knelt down on his front legs.

As they attempted to lift the man, a groan escaped from his lips. Aine couldn't dwell on his displeasure at being moved. Snow continued to fall rapidly. The wind dusted their clothing and face with large flakes, making their progress more difficult. With extreme effort, they managed to finally drag the man across the back of Drust.

Aine moved to the front of the horse while her brother kept firm hands on the man. Effortlessly, the horse rose to standing.

"Thank ye, Drust. We must make our way slowly out of the forest. Or—" She peered at her brother, hoping his power extended further. "Can ye move them both back to the stables?"

Keegan eyed her skeptically. "Currently, my skill is transporting one. If I risk sending them both back, the man might slip to his demise. In truth, using this much power weakens me."

Sweeping her gaze to Etain, she motioned for the wolfhound to take the lead. "Ye must show us the safest and quickest path to home, my friend."

The animal lumbered forward. Aine pulled the hood of her cloak over her head and grabbed the reins of the horse. The north wind slapped viciously, leaving its bitter sting across her cheeks. She clenched her jaw as she urged the animal upward. Whispering soothing words to her mount, they made slow progress along a path that had seen better days. Rocks, broken branches, and slush from the snow littered the ground.

Giving a gentle tug, she led the horse onward through the forest. During their journey, they were forced to halt several times. The man either groaned or attempted to wake. Keegan kept a firm hand on his backside, assuring him all would be well and to rest.

Regardless of her brother's thoughts on this foolish course of action, he made no attempt to leave the man.

As the wind blew more snow in their direction, Aine began to worry Etain was lost, unable to seek a clear direction out of the forest. She gritted her teeth as she held firm to the reins of the horse, urging Drust to continue moving forward.

Whispering prayers of protection and guidance, Aine squinted within the white blur of the tempest.

"Halt!" Keegan ordered.

Frustrated, Aine let the reins drop and turned toward her brother. "We cannot delay our progress."

Another groan emanated from the man.

"He will not calm," complained her brother.

The bite of the north wind chilled her bones as she considered another strategy. "Let us switch places."

"Nae. Ye are not tall enough," he argued, wiping a hand over his nose.

Challenging him, she pressed, "Let me try."

Without waiting for a response, Aine swept past her brother and went to the other side of the horse. While she stood on her tiptoes, she raised her hand and pressed her palm gently on the man's head. "Hear me, do not fight so. I am attempting to get ye to shelter. Relax," she soothed.

Soon, the man quieted, and Aine let out a sigh of relief.

"I shall remain by his side," she announced, removing her hand. Aine lifted her gaze to find her brother glowering at her. He finally relented and gave her a curt nod.

Onward they traveled without any more difficulties. When they finally reached the edge of the forest, Aine could see the castle below. Even though snow swirled in a tumult around the large structure, she could make out the shadows of the stone tower. Wood smoke drifted on the breeze, and she shivered once again.

Ye should have remained in the warmth of your bed, instead of wandering into a dark and frigid forest to make another unwise wish.

The horse jerked along the path, startling Aine out of her thoughts.

There was no time to ponder her previous actions. She needed to focus. The injured man required her tending. Her hand, now numb with cold, remained on the man's arm for reassurance and calm.

Wiping her other hand over her nose, Aine ignored the biting pain of cold and trudged forward.

****

The stirrings of far-off music, followed by a woman's soothing voice, eased the burning pain within his head. Attempting to open his eyes proved more difficult. The searing agony pierced his mind like a thousand blades. Even to speak one word proved unsuccessful. Why couldn't he move? Had he been in a battle? Frustration coiled within his body as he struggled to remember.

Then he recalled the lass's smile. A beacon of light within the flurry of snow and darkness. He longed to take her into his arms and kiss her smile.

And the next moment, pain slammed inside his head with the force of a hammer.

Determined to stay calm, he took in deep breaths, willing his limbs to do his bidding. He would not succumb to the abyss of sleep until he knew what had happened. Moments ticked by in agonizing torment, but he wouldn't relent. When his fingers flexed, he almost wanted to shout for joy.

Once again, he attempted to open his eyes. Sunlight slashed across the furs from an open shutter. He blinked in an effort to focus. Was this his chamber? Or not? Nothing appeared familiar, and yet…

Images flashed in a swirling mass of colors as he tried to bring together one memory. More pain surged into him, and he squeezed his eyes shut, letting out a groan of protest.

"Sweet Mother Danu, ye have wakened," announced the soothing female voice. Footsteps padded to his side, and she swiped a gentle finger over his brow.

Instantly, the pain subsided to a dull ache. Upon opening his eyes, he marveled at the beauty hovering above him—the same lass from the forest. His heart drummed rapidly against his chest. He swallowed, gazing deeply into eyes that mirrored the lavender fields in summer. He couldn't recall ever seeing such beauty. With great effort, he lifted his hand and brushed his fingers across one cheek. "Your name?"

Her smile lit up her entire face. "I am called Aine." Tilting her head to the side, she asked, "And what shall I call *ye*?"

His brow knitted together. His name a mystery like all his other memories. Uncertain how to respond, he dropped his hand. "I…I do not ken."

A shadow of concern flashed within her eyes. "Can ye not recall anything?"

"Truthfully? Nae." *Only your smile.*

Tapping a finger against her full lips, she confessed, "Ye did take an awful bashing to the head from my brother."

"Am I the enemy?" he asked harshly, slowly glancing around the chamber in search of his weapon. Nothing, not even a small blade resided anywhere. *Though would ye recognize your own sword?*

Grasping his arm, she quickly added, "Ye must not find fault with my brother. He was simply protecting

31

me."

"Ye have not answered my question," he responded dryly, returning his gaze to hers.

Aine slipped her hand free from his arm, and he felt the loss instantly. She clasped her hands together. "We have nae enemies here. Ye are a...*traveler*. I reckon we shall call ye Alex. 'Tis a strong name."

"*Alex*," he echoed, turning the name over in his mind. "I believe ye have chosen well. I like the name."

Moving to a small table, she poured some liquid into a cup. Alex studied her movements. Her mass of curls reminded him of honey as they floated down her back, bouncing with each sway of her hips. He clenched his hands tighter. Lust slammed into him, and he quickly looked away. *How hard did your brother hit me? And if I'm not the enemy, why did he feel the need to protect ye?*

Returning to his side, the lass held the cup to his lips while supporting his head with her other hand. "Drink. This will help in your healing."

Alex knew one thing. He disliked being weak. And her nearness overpowered his senses. She smelled like the woods and honey. "Ale or mead?"

A snort escaped from those luscious lips. "*Broth* for healing, though I am unsure if this will aid in your memories."

Hesitant to take a sip, he asked, "Are ye a healer?"

She laughed, filling the chamber with her musical sound.

Alex was sorely tempted to smile but refrained and drank deeply from the cup. Sweet liquid mixed with herbs trickled down his throat, warming him completely. When he finished, Alex nodded in thanks and rested his head against the pillows.

After placing the cup back on the table, Aine dragged a chair to his bedside. "I am not a healer but do have knowledge of herbs. My uncle made the healing brew for ye."

Regarding her skeptically, Alex pondered where the brother and uncle were at the moment. Leaving the lass in a chamber with a closed door and a stranger made him consider two options. Either they considered him too weak to be a threat to Aine, or they assumed he would remain honorable.

For all I ken, I am a bastard who takes women by force. He grimaced. Regardless of his loss of memories, a part of him realized this was not true. Never would he take any woman who did not come willingly. If only he could recall one woman. Closing his eyes, he concentrated on a simple recollection. Emptiness greeted him, yet without any more pain. He grunted in frustration and wiped a hand across his brow.

"Are ye still with pain?"

Her question snapped him out of his thoughts, and Alex opened his eyes. "Nae. What has happened to my tunic and cloak?"

"Soon ye will have your strength. Perchance after another night's rest—"

"Another night's rest?" he interrupted, attempting to sit up in the bed. "How long have I been asleep?"

Standing abruptly, Aine pressed him back onto the furs. "Ye must regain your strength and not force your body to do what the mind has ordered. Your clothing was muddy, and the cloak required stitching. My uncle has kindly provided ye with trews."

Alex gaped at her. Did she not understand his words? "How *long*?" His frustration made the question

33

harsher than he intended.

"Three nights," answered the man standing in the doorway.

"By the hounds! Three nights?" His voice echoed off the stones within the chamber.

Ignoring his outburst, Aine crossed the room to the man's side. "Is this not good news that he has woke from the deep sleep, Uncle?"

Keeping his focus on Alex, the man affirmed, "Aye. We must offer up prayers for his swift healing."

Uneasy over the man's scrutiny, Alex demanded, "Will someone kindly assist me to sitting? I have nae desire to spend another full day in bed."

The man moved toward him.

"Nae, Uncle Eamon," pleaded Aine. "He must rest until fully healed."

"Our guest has resided long enough in this chamber." Glancing sharply at her, he added, "And ye have as well. Go break your fast and then get some rest."

The lass bit her lower lip as if debating a response to her uncle's order. She began to tap her foot.

Her uncle clasped his hands behind his back. "Is there something else ye want to say, Aine?"

She blew out a disturbed breath and shook her head. "Nae." As she made her way out of the chamber, she peered over her shoulder and gave Alex another beaming smile.

When the door closed behind her, the man unclasped his hands. Heaving a heavy sigh, he stepped near the side of the bed. "Would ye care to sit in the chair by the hearth?"

Relief coursed through Alex. "Gladly."

Though weakness plagued him, Alex managed with

the man's assistance to get off the bed and slowly make his way to the chair. Raking a hand through his hair, he tried to find the wound. His fingers encountered a small lump but nothing as serious to keep him abed for three nights.

Eamon leaned against the wall near the hearth. "I am sorry for the actions of my nephew."

Alex required answers not apologies. "Can ye tell me why he felt it necessary to render a blow to my head?"

The man took a seat across from Alex. Settling back, he folded his arms over his chest. "Keegan can be protective of his sister. I deem he felt ye would bring her harm."

"What were they doing out in the forest at night?"

The man shrugged. "What were ye doing there?"

Clenching his jaw, Alex sought to give the man an answer. Utter emptiness greeted him when he tried to snatch a memory. He pounded a fist onto the arm of the chair. "I have nae answer."

The fire in the hearth snapped, echoing Alex's mood.

The man nodded slowly. "Until ye can recall your memories, 'tis best ye remain with us. Furthermore, ye will be treated as our guest."

"Where am I?"

Eamon leaned forward and braced his forearms on his thighs. "Ye are in Castle Taloch in the Great Glen."

Frowning, Alex rubbed a hand through several days' growth of beard. No recollection of the place stirred any memory in him. "Can ye not ask in the next village for information about me, or if I have kin?"

Eamon rose. "There are nae others nearby. I will

have someone bring ye food and fresh clothing."

Uneasiness coursed through Alex's veins. *Nae others?* How far had he journeyed? What about his horse? Supplies? His sword? With each new question, another slipped through his thoughts.

Though his mind barren of his previous life, Alex would wager any coin the man had lied.

Chapter Four

"When ye become weak, strike out the offending emotion with your blade." ~MacFhearguis Motto

After spending another day confined to the small chamber, Alex judged he was able to venture outside. Fresh clothing was given the day before, along with his cloak. As he stepped out of the room, he surveyed the details of the dwelling and slowly made his way down a small section of wooden stairs. Striding with purpose toward the entrance, he paused by an open doorway into a sizable room. Books and parchments littered a large desk near a wide arched window. Yet what captured his attention was a harp gracing one of the chairs near the hearth.

Alex recalled the luring strings of music and *her* voice. He peered inside, hoping Aine would be there but found only another table and chairs along the wall. He shrugged away the disappointment.

When cold pressure nudged against his hand, Alex dropped his gaze to a large wolfhound. She proceeded to settle herself next to him with a somber expression.

Arching a brow, he dipped his head toward the animal. "Greetings. Am I blocking the path to your warmth?"

"*Etain* is always ready to return to the haven of a good fire. Her bones are ancient, but that doesn't stop her from treading out into the snow to see the other animals."

Alex turned at the sound of the man's voice. He'd thought himself a large man, but this man loomed over him. He stood at the entrance of the castle with his hands fisted on his hips, blocking what little sunlight streaked through the open door.

A sliver of familiarity wove through Alex. Eyes the color of another stared with intent back at him. *Ye must be Keegan. The brother.* He ruffled his fingers over the wolfhound's coarse fur while maintaining his sight on the man. Whereas Keegan's height might rival few, his sister was small in size.

"A fine name for this warrior animal," Alex remarked.

The man's features softened. "Aye, given she has fought to maintain her leadership over the others."

"Others?" echoed Alex.

"Dogs, horses, goats. The list is varied and endless." The man dropped his hands to his sides. "They are her...*children.*"

"Interesting," he mused. "Speaking of horses, can ye show me the direction of the stables. I want to inspect my horse. Ye are Keegan, aye? I see the resemblance from your sister."

A flash of irritation shone briefly in the man's eyes. "Aye," he acknowledged slowly. Turning around, Keegan strode briskly outside.

"And my horse?" demanded Alex, rushing after him.

"Ye were fortunate we found him in time. The snows were heavy," snapped Keegan, darting around a group of ducks being driven across the muddy, slush-covered ground by a young lass.

"I can assure ye—" Halting midstride, Alex wiped a hand over his brow. *What was the animal's name? Will I even recognize my own horse?* He clenched his jaw, attempting to draw forth a name or memory.

"Are ye coming?" shouted Keegan.

Alex jerked his head up and resumed his path forward. When he stepped inside the large structure, his gaze roamed around the interior. Noting the appearance of three horses in their stalls, he held back the curse he wanted to fling out. Not one of them did he recognize. He blew out a frustrated breath.

Standing against a wooden gate, Keegan surveyed him sharply.

Alex shifted his stance. He gave no care what the man thought of him. "Which one is mine?"

"My sister has shared your loss of memories." He pointed to last stall. "The black *beast* is yours."

Hesitantly, Alex moved toward the horse. He raised an outstretched hand. Dark, watchful eyes regarded him. "Forgive me. I have forgotten your name, along with my past. Have we journeyed far together?"

The horse nudged his wet nose against his palm.

Chuckling softly, Alex beamed. "So are ye truly a beast, my friend?"

"'Tis what my sister declared when she fed him oats this morn," confessed Keegan.

Alex stroked his fingers down the glossy mane of the animal. "Do ye prefer *apples*?"

The horse whinnied in response.

Keegan snorted. "Then apples ye shall have." Moving away from the gate, he paused at the entrance. "Ye could have stated this earlier, *Beast*."

"Is the man daft? Ye cannot speak your preference

for food," muttered Alex.

"According to my sister, she did ask the animal," corrected Keegan, adding, "yet he remained silent."

Curious, Alex asked, "Where is Aine?"

When no response greeted him, Alex gave a final pat to the animal. Striding quickly outside, he came to an abrupt halt. Keegan made long strides across the bailey, stopping to chat with a passing lad or to assist a young lass with her basket of herbs.

Alex remained rooted in his stance. Slowly, he gazed around the area. Children darted across the bailey, each carrying a parcel or basket. As he frowned upon the scene, he pondered why there were no older men and women. Taking a few steps, he glanced at the round central tower. The archway leading into the castle held no portcullis, and he narrowed his eyes.

Nae elders. Nae guards. Where in the Gods' name am I?

Since Keegan continued to ignore him, Alex thought to survey the large keep on his own. Many of the young ones gave him a broad smile or let out a giggle in passing. When one lass dipped a curtsy, Alex blinked in surprise. Before he had a chance to correct her, she dashed away from him.

Continuing on his journey, he'd stop every so often to inspect a side entrance into the castle or attempt to catch one of the young lads so to direct him on the whereabouts of Aine. As he passed by a large garden, the scents of rosemary drifted by him. Even though the day was brisk, sunlight streamed down in wonderous warmth on his shoulders.

Sounds of the smithy beckoned him forward. As his steps led him closer, Alex halted at the vision before him.

Poised over the anvil, Aine leveled the hammer against the metal with strength that stunned Alex. For one so small, she wielded the hammer with fierceness. Beads of sweat trickled down her cheek, smudged with the grime of her work. She gave no regard to her appearance, or him, while she continued. Studying her profile, he fought the urge to pick up a cloth and wipe away the moisture along with the dirt from her ivory skin. Her honeyed hair was woven into two braids and wrapped around her head like a crown of silken jewels.

Leaning against an oak tree, Alex regarded her in fascination. The smithy stood as a place reserved for men. This he knew. Then why would a woman accept a position in the castle fashioning weapons?

Aine blew out a curse, and he smiled in response.

The woman was mesmerizing. Captivating. He folded his arms over his chest, content to remain hidden and watch her in secret. When something nudged his thigh, Alex quickly moved to the side. "By the hounds," he hissed out in surprise at the sudden appearance of the wolfhound. "I thought I left ye by the warm fire."

"Etain has taken to ye," announced Aine while inspecting the blade in front of her. She darted him a glance.

Alex straightened his tunic and stepped forward. "She moves silently for one so large. Are ye sure she does not belong to the Fae?"

The blade slipped from Aine's fingers onto the anvil with a large clang. Her eyes grew wide as she turned away from Alex. "'Tis folly. She is only a dog," she mumbled, quickly retrieving the blade and disappearing from his view.

Concerned, Alex followed her. Once he entered

inside the forge, his eyes adjusted to the dimly lit enclosure. He observed the other blades of various sizes strewn out on a wooden table along with horseshoes. A glint of light at the end of the table drew his attention. He steadily made his way to the stunning circular brooches. Their gilded edges were carved with delicate knotwork. Tracing his finger along the smooth surface of one, he marveled at the craftmanship. Surely she had assistance.

He lifted his gaze to the woman.

While Aine kept her back to him, Alex noted her rigid stance. Unsure on what to do, he clasped his hands behind his back. "Did ye make all of these?"

Clenching her fists, she turned around. Wariness reflected back at him within those lavender eyes. "Does it matter?"

"'Tis a simple question," he remarked.

Her eyes narrowed. "Because I am a *woman*, aye?"

Alex's gaze roamed over her face and traveled down the length of her. "Most assuredly." He took a step forward. "But that is not why I asked the question."

Bright splotches appeared on her cheeks. She swallowed but kept her gaze locked with his. "Aye. 'Tis all my work. Mine alone," she confessed.

"Who has taught ye this skill?"

She lifted her chin. "My father and Gordon. I now share the forge with Gordon since my father's death."

Arching a brow, Alex reached around her, inhaling the woman's scent. As his fingers touched the cool surface of a blade, he brought forth the small dirk and lifted it up to the candlelight. "Incredible craftmanship."

Aine's eyes widened in shock. "Ye approve of my work?" Her question barely a whisper.

"Why would I not?"

"Because I should be learning how to sew, tending to the gardens, and making a simple bannock," she grumbled, glancing beyond him.

"I favor bread over any bannock," he chided.

Returning her attention to him, she grabbed his arm. "Ye can recall something from your past? Is there more?"

Her smile beamed like starlight on a winter's night, and Alex became entranced. Why had he become fascinated with this woman? His gut clenched and his mouth dried whenever he entered her presence. Had he not spent much time around women? Or worse, married to one? He quickly banished the thought. Alex could not dwell on what he was unable to remember.

"Nae, I simply ken," he replied. Though there were things inside of him he understood—from withholding his trust to realizing what he liked to eat and drink. And also, the night he ventured along a snowy path between giant oak trees which led him to this place.

He gazed down at Aine. "Do ye think ye can make a dirk for me? Apparently, I have lost mine along my journey."

Her hands twisted within the folds of her gown. "Ye...ye did not have a dirk but carried a sword," she confessed softly.

I believe 'tis the first truth I have heard since waking.

Conflicting emotions battled within Alex. Why did these people find him a threat? Was he the enemy? Or were they to him? "Does this mean ye will not be making one for me? Do ye think I am a threat to ye and the others?" asked Alex, determined to find out more from the lass.

She snatched the blade from his fingers with a swiftness that surprised him. "Most men would not want a weapon forged by a woman. And your sword is magnificent."

Intrigued, he pressed further. "Do ye find me like *most* men, Aine? How many have ye known?" Though the thought of Aine being with any man made his insides twist.

She shrugged and deposited the blade back onto the table. When her body brushed against his, she shuddered.

Alex took a hesitant step back. Did he repel her with his presence? He scratched the beard on his face. *By the Gods, ye must see me as a brute suffering from lust while within your company.*

Sighing heavily, he asked, "Where is my sword?"

Pointing to a darkened corner, she replied, "'Tis there. I merely wished to study the hilt and steel. 'Tis not often we have travelers."

Alex walked over and retrieved his sword. Striding to the entrance, he studied the hilt in the gray light of day by running his thumb down the side. A lion was carved into the wood on one side, and on the other, a falcon. His vison blurred as he struggled to bring forth any image.

When nothing of the past greeted him, he squeezed his eyes shut. Frustration seethed within him.

A gentle hand touched his arm. "Give your mind time to heal. Your memories will return when the Goddess believes ye are ready."

Turning toward her soothing voice, Alex opened his eyes and laughed bitterly. "The old Gods do not listen to me."

Her lips twitched with mirth as she dropped her hand. "I deem the Gods and Goddesses listen to everyone. If ye still desire, I shall be honored to fashion a dirk for ye."

Glancing sideways at her, Alex nodded slowly. "My thanks, Aine."

Reaching outward with her finger, she tapped the lion on the hilt. "Great courage to carry this animal with ye, along with the wisdom and cunningness of the falcon on the other side. I fathom ye are a great leader."

Alex drew back and lowered the sword by his side. "Any *great* leader would not have gone unaccompanied without guards into a tempest of a snowstorm."

Again, she shrugged dismissively. "Since ye do not ken all the details, I would wait to make a judgement."

Before he could respond, loud shouting, followed by the appearance of several goats halted any further conversation. The animals were intent on escaping the clutches of two children who were running toward them, scampering between the trees.

"Do not let them enter the forge," warned Aine, taking a warrior stance in front of the entrance.

Alex propped his sword against a wooden pillar. "Do ye have any food inside?"

She snapped her gaze to him. "A dried bannock and an apple. Did ye not break your fast?"

"Nae, but 'tis not why I require them. Go fetch both," he ordered.

Staring at him for several heartbeats, Aine swiftly complied. She returned with the food items and handed them to him. "Is your plan to bribe the unruly animals with food? They do not trust anyone, even those with food."

Unsure how to explain, Alex strode forward to the nearest tree. Crouching down against the hard bark, he held out his offerings. Giving a short two-burst whistle, he waited.

One of the children darted in front of him.

"Take up a position by Aine," barked out Alex.

The lad skidded to a halt. Giving him a curt nod, he dashed over to Aine.

Aine let out a snort of laughter and folded her arms over her chest. "The beasties are stubborn animals and do not come to anyone."

Alex arched a brow and then gave another two-burst whistle.

Within moments, the goats trotted over to his side and proceeded to nibble on the food within his outstretched hands.

The lass halted before him. "By the Goddess, ye can speak to them." Her eyes grew wide along with a broad smile which revealed a missing tooth.

Alex chuckled low. "Nae, lass. 'Tis the first thought I recalled when dealing with surly animals."

"Hamish and Cara, secure these goats and return them to their pen," demanded Aine, coming to his side.

After the children tethered the goats together with Alex's assistance, he stood.

Aine shielded her eyes in the soft light of day as she watched them depart. "Cara is correct, Alex. Not one person has been able to tame those wild ones since they arrived here." She waved a hand outward. "Even Etain has taken to ye, and she is difficult to please."

"First ye thought me a leader, now one who talks to animals?" Alex brushed a hand across his neck.

Turning slowly to meet his questioning gaze, she responded, "Why not both? A great leader who can charm the animals and people to do his bidding."

For a moment, Alex contemplated the possibility. Then swiftly shrugged the thought aside.

I am not a man who charms with words. This much he understood about himself.

Chapter Five

"Great wisdom is never fully attained, even at the end of a long life." ~Fae Lore

Plucking at an irritating loose thread on the sleeve of her gown, Aine tried to maintain her focus on the conversation between Elder Rory and her uncle. How she wanted to stomp her foot in frustration. But then they would see her lack of patience and manners. Ever since Uncle Eamon had called her from the forge, she had attempted to squelch the uneasiness humming throughout her body.

When she entered the great hall, the air grew chilly, even with the blazing heat from the hearth. Her uncle barely acknowledged her. Instead, he gave her a warning look—one she knew well. Even Elder Rory seemed displeased by her appearance as he paced in front of the hearth.

Aine kept silent. When her uncle pulled out a chair, she reluctantly took a seat. Yet after an hour of intense discussions between the two men over her actions, she struggled to listen and remain calm. She yearned to offer her own opinions and give her account. If they refused to listen to her, she'd return to the forge and begin work on the dirk for Alex.

Her thoughts drifted to the strange traveler. He appeared content to wander the grounds while she hurried after her uncle's summons. Alex stirred something inside her—warm, confusing, exciting, and different. There had been other men who ventured within their realm for business with her uncle. Usually, they were traders who were allowed to journey through their land. Or the traveler whose purpose happened to be destined for another from the castle.

Yet only one man made Aine's heart pound fiercely. Her palms tingled whenever Alex drew near. Was he the one to take her away from this haven? To show her the Scotland of humans? Or once on the other side, would he abandon her in his world?

She sighed and rubbed a hand across her brow.

"Did ye not train her to leave her magic in the ground?" demanded Rory. "She has brought forth a man into this haven. In doing so, harm has befallen him. Furthermore, the man is trapped here until we can determine how to send him back through."

Aine turned her displeasure toward Elder Rory. *How dare ye assume I did not have the proper training. And Keegan gave him the injury. Why is he not here?*

Her uncle's jaw tightened. "Ye ken Aine has a will of her own. Her power is strong. I reckon Aine misunderstood her intentions."

Rory dismissed his words with a wave of his hand. "All are powerful here. Even her brother has respect for the magic and does not wield the power for his satisfaction. If ye had known of her rebellious will, ye should have bound her powers until a certain age."

Her lip curled in disgust. *Keegan is not so innocent with his powers. Ye should watch him more closely. And I am two and twenty, not some wee lass!*

"Ye ken we do not harbor the old ways here, Rory,"

argued her uncle. "If we restrained her powers, then she would not learn the valuable lessons for the outside world. Even ye must consider the consequences of lessons not learned."

Bind my powers? For the love of the Goddess! 'Tis an outrage! "I am not a child," she mumbled, yanking more on the thread, leaving her gown unraveling and her insides churning with fury.

All conversation halted, and both men glared at her.

Her face heated at the intensity of their unspoken thoughts. She didn't think they would hear her. Once again, she failed in her training, especially in front of an elder. "My apologies. The words tumbled free before I could stop them."

"*Aine*," warned her uncle.

Rory narrowed his eyes and shook his head. His features then softened as he leaned against the table. "Since ye are unable to remain *silent*, I welcome your words on this predicament."

Welcome? Aine almost let out a snort. Almost. Straightening in her chair, she clasped her hands together. "Aye, I parted the veil. Did I intend to do so?" She shook her head. "*Nae*. Yet ye and my uncle are arguing over an event which has already occurred. We must welcome this traveler into our home and assist in the mending of his memories. Since I brought him forth, I shall bear the responsibility of his healing."

Swallowing, Aine dared to tempt their anger further by adding, "Did ye not consider the Goddess wished this to happen?"

"Are ye on speaking terms with Mother Danu?" snapped her uncle, gripping the back of one of the chairs.

Embarrassed by his question, Aine glanced away.

"All speak with Mother Danu, Eamon," uttered Rory softly. "Perchance the lass is correct."

Snapping her attention to the elder, Aine held her breath. *He believes me.*

Her uncle moved to her side. "However, have ye considered the man might have family? A wife? Children? Ye do not ken who he is, Aine. Can ye be content to travel beyond the veil and make a life on your own?"

Aine's insides twisted like the gnarled roots of the giant oak sacred to them. What if Alex was merely the guardian to escort her to the other side into Scotland? What if he abandoned her there? She'd be forced to make a life on her own. Alone. Her resolve hardened. The future—her future had yet to be written. "Then if it's the will of the Goddess, I cannot argue or complain."

The elder crossed his arms over his chest. "I ken the man. He has nae wife or children."

Aine let out the breath she had held back. Hope flared like the stars in the night sky. She grasped her uncle's hand. "'Tis the fate of the Goddess."

Eamon gave the elder a skeptical glance. "Ye could have mentioned this earlier to me. My fear is for Aine when the man recovers his memories. I did not want her to suffer if this traveler is not meant to take her across. Is he a good man? Does he ken ye are a Fenian warrior? What belief does the man follow—the new religion or the old?"

All questions Aine burned to ask as well.

Rory dropped his hands to his side. "I shall say this and nae more. Aye, the man is honorable, and he is nae threat to our beliefs." His brow furrowed in thought. "I deem it best I remain here as a guest to oversee his progress. In time, his mind will recover, and he will recognize me. 'Tis wise to let the natural healing progress."

Rising slowly, Aine smiled at the elder. "Thank ye."

Rory laughed bitterly. "Do not be so hasty in your thanks, Aine, especially when he does recover. Nae man likes to be fooled."

Reaching for a jug, Eamon poured ale into two cups, the contents sloshing over the rim and onto the table. "What a bee's nest ye have stirred, Aine."

"Can ye at least share his name with us?" she asked, shoving aside the elder and her uncle's words of warning.

"Ye ask a question ye already ken the answer, Aine Fraser," he responded tersely. "Your insight with the man's horse has already revealed his name."

She chewed on her bottom lip. "I meant his surname."

The elder shoved away from the table. "MacFhearguis. Alex MacFhearguis."

"He is kin to one of the Dragon Knights?" she blurted out.

"His younger brother. Furthermore, the day of reckoning will come," warned Rory.

Her eyes widened. "Should I be wary of Alex?"

Rory stepped near her. "Aye, ye should be. The man is ruthless, cunning, and has nae tolerance for betrayal. I have shared more than intended with ye. Since ye have tampered with his and your strings of destiny, the outcome might not be one ye yearned for, Aine."

The flames snapped within the hearth. A shiver of uncertainty slipped within her as she shifted her attention to the sparks dancing upward. *The path I take will be my choice—good or bad—this is my fate.* Aine had always known another life awaited her beyond the veil. This home merely a shelter of learning. Adventures beckoned her beyond the great forest.

Slowly, she returned her attention to Rory. "As for Alex MacFhearguis, who are we to argue with the plans of the Goddess? Surely if he were not meant to come forth, she wouldn't have allowed him to venture on through. Aye?"

The man's eyes flashed with silver. "Do not tempt to assume ye understand the will of Mother Danu."

Before Aine could respond, the doors to the great hall swung open.

Alex halted his stride at the entrance. "Forgive the interruption. I thought to quench my throat with a cup of ale."

"Sweet Goddess, ye have not had any food or drink this morn," gasped Aine, recalling earlier his mentioning of not breaking his fast. She dashed to his side.

Alex's expression softened. "I could have eaten the apple and dried bannock instead of giving them to the goats."

Smiling, Aine waved him on over to a table. "A guest should not have to eat stale food. I shall go gather some bread, cheese, and fruit."

Shifting his stance, he said, "Nae. Show me where I can find the kitchens. I'll tend to my meal. I do not want to disrupt your discussions."

"Aine is correct. Ye are a guest here at Castle Taloch," Rory called out, approaching by her side.

Noting the wariness in Alex, she quickly added, "This is our Elder."

"*Elder?*" echoed Alex, giving the man a dark glance.

"He appears nae older than me."

Rory barked out in laughter and then swiftly composed himself. "I can see ye are an observant man, Alex. The people have taken to calling me thus for my wisdom."

Eamon strode forth and handed Alex a cup of ale. "'Tis the truth. Rory MacGregor has journeyed to countless lands. His knowledge is vast." The man waved his hand outward. "As ye have most surely witnessed, there are a great number of children who roam the castle. They are the orphaned ones left behind from the death of their parents, or battles fought and lost. Often, the children are forgotten after birth."

Alex's brow furrowed. "Where is their chieftain? 'Tis his responsibility to give shelter and find others to aid in their rearing."

"There is none," confessed Rory. "Eamon oversees the children's tutoring with assistance from Aine, Keegan, and a few others."

Taking a sip of the ale, Alex regarded Aine's uncle over the rim of his cup. "'Tis a heady responsibility. Ye also appear nae older than Rory."

Silence descended within the hall.

Ye are shrewd, Alex MacFhearguis. 'Tis another quality about ye. Aine grew weary of the banter between all the men. "Please take a seat near the hearth, Alex," she pleaded, reaching for his arm.

Amber eyes flecked with green stared back at her. The look he gave her made her insides tremble.

"If ye so insist," he acknowledged softly.

She blinked as if coming out of a daze. Ignoring Rory and her uncle, Aine led the man to a table along the wall near the hearth. "I shall return with food and a fresh jug of ale."

While making quick strides out of the hall, Aine kept her attention fixed on the entrance. She dared not look at her uncle or Rory. Would they be able to notice her uneasiness around the man?

As she made her way past them, Rory's words made her pause.

"Remember my warning, Aine," he whispered to her.

Giving the elder a curt nod, she swiftly departed.

When she entered the kitchens, she hastily collected a few items and placed them on a trencher. Snatching a loaf of fresh bread from a table by the ovens, she prayed Rowena would not be displeased. The cook had strict rules about taking food without her permission.

Footsteps padded behind her. She stole a glance over her shoulder and breathed a sigh of relief at the intruder. "Are your chores finished, Cara?"

"Aye," confirmed the young girl, pulling out a stool. "The goats are secured in their pen." She seated herself across from Aine. "Who is the traveler? Is he the one everyone says will take ye away?"

Filling a jug with fresh ale, Aine managed to keep her voice calm when she replied, "The *traveler's* name is Alex. And I am unsure to his *or* my plans."

Cara twirled her braid between her fingers. "The animals like him."

After placing the jug down, Aine reached for the girl's hand. "Aye, they have spoken to me as well. He has a kind heart."

Cara's lip trembled. "They speak of ye leaving. And once ye depart, ye can never return."

Aine squeezed her tiny fingers. "Until the man's

memories return, no one is leaving this castle. And we all prepare for the day to venture out beyond the veil. Even ye will take the journey."

The lass trembled under her touch and cast her gaze beyond Aine. The lavender color now replaced by silver—one Aine knew well. The eyes of the Seer shone brightly within Cara. The young lass never knew when the vision would take hold of her. She merely went quiet while her eyes shimmered.

Aine dropped her hand and stood back.

Though the air cooled within the kitchens, beads of moisture trickled down the back of Aine's neck. Respect kept her rooted in place while she waited for the Seer within the young lass to impart her wisdom.

Cara's voice took on a somber tone. "The land has been torn apart." The girl shuddered before continuing. "The veil is shattered. To mend the rift between above and below can only be sewn together once. During the shortest day and longest night can ye weave the words of healing. Once spoken, ye cannot change what the stars have written. Ye cannot keep what is not given. When ye witness the appearance of the white stag who brings ye the white rose, the time of healing begins anew."

The young girl's head sagged forward on a sigh. "Head hurts."

What have I done? They were simply wishes under the stars. With a trembling hand, Aine reached across the table and dragged a jug of water to her. Filling one of the cups, she held it outward, waiting for the vision to lessen within Cara.

"Here, drink this," urged Aine.

Rubbing her eyes, Cara met Aine's troubled gaze. The lass took the cup and drank deeply. When she had enough, the girl handed the cup back to her. "Did ye understand the knowledge?"

Aine had no intention of worrying the lass. Turning away, she placed the cup on the table and gathered the food items and jug of ale. "Aye," she lied.

"Should we give an account to Uncle Eamon?" Cara's question was laced with concern.

When Aine returned her attention to her, she gave the girl a weak smile. "Nae. Let us not trouble him with this new vision. Moreover, Elder Rory is here."

Cara nodded slowly.

Before departing the kitchens, Aine placed a feather-like kiss on the girl's troubled frown. "Stay here and wait for Rowena. Have her make ye a tonic of elderberry and peppermint."

The girl's features brightened. "I am helping her with the damson tarts."

Aine's mouth twitched in humor. "Better ye than me."

Cara's nosed wrinkled in disdain. "Are ye sure ye used damsons the last time ye baked for us?"

"They were bitter," acknowledged Aine, shifting the trencher in her arm and heading for the great hall. Her thoughts went to the words the lass had spoken during her vision. *What can't I keep? Alex?* Her steps briefly faltered. She couldn't dwell on questions now and banished the unease coursing through her.

"Even the animals did not like them!" shouted Cara.

"'Tis a wonder Rowena allows me in the kitchens," grumbled Aine as she made her way down the corridor.

Once inside the hall, she deposited everything on the table. Both her uncle and Rory had seated themselves across from Alex. The conversation flowed around the hall as if old friends had gathered.

After giving fresh ale to all the men, she took a chair beside Alex and pushed the trencher of food his way.

Eamon continued to talk about the crops and food storage for the winter that would sustain the people here. Although Rory gave his account on a section of the roof in the northern end that required mending, he welcomed any advice from the man. Alex observed and gave his counsel. Was he drawing on his experience? He responded as one who shared his opinion and thoughts often. Aine watched in fascination while her uncle and Rory discussed needs for the long winter months ahead.

When Alex tore off a piece of bread, she noticed his gaze searching through the trencher.

"Is there something else ye require?" she asked, hoping this light fare would sustain the man until the evening meal.

He arched a dark brow. "Blade to cut the cheese?"

Aine retrieved the small *sgian dubh* from her belt on her side. "My apologies. I forgot to bring one with the food."

"There is nae need to make amends." When he reached for her blade, his warm fingers brushed against hers. His gaze held hers. The heat from his touch seared into her hand and up Aine's arm.

Instantly, she drew her hand back into her lap. Her heart thumped wildly against her chest, and Aine fought the urge to cool her burning cheeks with her hand.

As the men continued with their conversation, Aine understood what they were attempting with Alex. They hoped to stir some kind of image from deep within his mind. And yet, nothing came forth. Perchance they could ken each other without the knowledge of their pasts—his and hers. Would the man find contempt when he learned the truth? Would he scorn her and flee back to his home?

"I have extended my visit here," Rory announced. "Would ye like to inspect the roof and surrounding area of the castle in the morning?"

"No training in the lists?" inquired Alex dryly. "Are your lands secure that ye do not require guards in the tower? And nae gate?"

Rory leaned forward. "I can assure ye all people are protected here. But if ye have need of showing us your skills, I accept your challenge."

Alex drummed his fingers on the rough wood. "My mind might be troubled, but my sword arm is strong."

"First light of dawn," declared Rory.

A smile twitched on Aine's mouth. She reached for the jug of ale and filled one of the cups. Taking a sip of the cool liquid, Aine settled back in her chair. Regarding Alex over the rim of her cup, she remained content to listen.

Regardless of the warning words from Cara's vision, I will not give ye back, Alex MacFhearguis. There is much to learn from ye. I shall keep my secrets, and ye are welcomed to do the same.

Chapter Six

"Strength, loyalty, and leadership. Qualities admirable in the lion and a chieftain." ~MacFhearguis Motto

Alex leaned against the wooden gate leading into the lists and watched the last star slipping from the sky. The stirrings of dawn slowly rose on a new day. Content to observe the first light entering, he mused on last evening's meal—one where many of the people had fought to sit near him. As the new visitor to the castle, they yearned to speak with him. Even without his past knowledge, he did his best to answer the questions they put forth. Yet there was one seated across from him who remained silent.

Aine Fraser.

Alex expected the lass to add her own questions to the many others presented to him during the meal. However, the lass merely observed. He felt her constant gaze—probing and heated. Only when her brother entered the hall did she start a conversation with another woman at the table, ignoring him for the duration of the meal.

"Why do ye haunt my thoughts? I am not the man ye should seek out, Aine," he whispered into the chilled morning air, while he gripped the hilt of his sword and inhaled deeply.

A hollow ache settled inside Alex. Why did he have this connection here? And why did he want to learn more about the lass with the mesmerizing eyes? His mind battled with his emotions each time she entered a room or strayed casually by with another. He had no desire to tempt his lustful beast further with one so young and innocent.

His life happened to be beyond this castle. One day his memories would return, and he'd depart.

Then there was Rory MacGregor. A faint recollection brushed over him when they met. Alex kept silent upon their meeting as he probed his mind for any singular remembrance. Nevertheless, he could not draw forth anything—not one bloody image. This emptiness plagued him. If they knew each other, surely the man would have acknowledged the kinship. *Unless we are enemies?*

"Are ye ready to train?" Rory drawled, coming alongside him.

"Should victory be claimed when the first man is thrown to the ground?" Alex shot back, unsheathing his sword.

Rory gave an exasperated snort. "Ye are confident against a man ye have not sparred against. I could have taken advantage of your casual stance and slammed ye to the ground."

Alex flashed him a dangerous look. "I smelled ye the moment ye stepped outside."

The man's lip curled. "I deem this is going to be battle of wits as well as strength of arm."

"Never underestimate your foe," challenged Alex, stepping aside and waving Rory onward into the lists.

Pausing at the entrance, Rory tilted his head to the

side. "'Tis true. But let us enjoy a good battle of strength. There is nae worry of snow to hinder our movements."

And in a blur of speed, Rory leveled his blade at him. But Alex proved swifter and not only deflected the attack but landed a blow to the man's jaw.

"Do ye think to maim me?" Rory protested. He rubbed a hand over his chin while entering into the center of the lists.

"Harsh words. Do ye fear the lasses will take a disliking to your bruised face?" mocked Alex.

Rory aimed his sword at him. "I charm them into my bed with words. And there is only *one* woman in my life, and she will not be pleased."

Stalking toward his foe, Alex shrugged. "I fear nae woman."

"And yet, ye cannot say for certain if one waits for ye?" challenged Rory.

"Nae," he growled, furious over his own doubts. "Enough! 'Tis a battle of blades not words."

Rory swung hard against Alex's raised sword. "I can assure ye, 'tis all I came out here to do this morn."

For the next half-hour, the clash of blades, blows to the body with fists, followed by grunts and curses flew out between the two men. Each intent on drawing forth blood. Regardless of Alex's strength, his foe was proving to be highly skilled. Alex embraced the brutal training, shoving aside his previous angst.

Leveling a fist into the man's side, Alex was rewarded with a kick to the knees, landing him on the ground. He swiftly rolled to the side and stood. Wiping blood from the cut on his brow, he shifted to the right, narrowly missing the blade's slash to his arm.

Blow after blow, they continued. Alex managed to

surprise the man when he landed another strike. This time his fist impacted Rory's nose, and the man staggered back. Blood spewed down his face. For a brief moment, Alex swore he saw the man's eyes flash with silver.

Taking advantage of Rory's momentary lapse to wipe away the blood, Alex charged forward and knocked him to the ground. When blood seeped into his eyes, causing his vision to blur, Alex tried to level his blade at the man's throat to claim victory. A flash of another battle image seared inside his thoughts and then swiftly fled. He tried to grasp the elusive memory, leaving him trapped between two worlds.

"Unless ye have nae need of this part of your body, I would suggest ye remove your sword from my chest," growled Rory, his breathing labored.

Alex blinked, focusing on his present situation. Glancing down at where his foe's blade remained poised inches from his balls, he roared with laughter. "Well done!" Dropping his sword to the ground, Alex held out his hand to the man.

Rory grimaced upon standing. "By the hounds of Cúchulainn! Ye came close to removing my heart!"

"Nae. To do so, would require me *shoving* my blade into your chest," chided Alex.

The thrill of physical activity coursed through his veins. After yanking his tunic over his head, Alex wiped the blood from his eyes with the garment. Striding across the lists to a large barrel, he submerged his head into the icy water. The cold, brittle sting eased the burning pain from the wound on his brow. Raising his head, he shook his head furiously while droplets of water flew around him.

He turned toward Rory, watching as the man cleansed the grime of their battle from his face. "Ye are a worthy foe."

The man pinched the bridge of his nose to stanch the blood and then dunked his head back into the barrel of water. When Rory withdrew from the water, he blinked several times. He scrubbed a hand over his face. "'Tis many moons since I have had the pleasure of a good fight."

Wrapping his tunic around his neck, Alex mused, "I cannot say the same."

"Give your mind time to heal," suggested Rory softly.

Alex frowned. "What if *time* is against me? For a brief moment, I saw another face and battle."

"Explain."

Shrugging, he confessed, "What if others depend on me? What if this man I saw is kin? Ye cannot fathom how this plagues me. Suppose I had a family? Or—"

"Certainly, your journey would not have led ye so far away," interrupted Rory. "The more ye fret, the more your mind will struggle." He clamped a hand on Alex's shoulder. "Allow the mind to heal, and all shall be revealed."

Alex winced from the pain.

Rory laughed and released his hold. "Forgive me."

Shaking his head, Alex responded, "I would welcome another round of blades tomorrow morn."

"And fists," add Rory.

While the men strolled to retrieve their weapons, a familiar lass stood within the shadows of the entrance. How long had she viewed their sparring? A frown creased her features, and Alex pondered what could have her troubled.

Curious, Alex glanced sideways at Rory. "Is Aine the oldest unmarried lass here?"

"Why?" responded the man dryly.

"Last evening, others suggested she is too old to marry."

Rory blew out a soft curse. "Certain lads, I presume?"

Alex nodded, picking up his sword from the ground.

"Though Aine and Keegan are the oldest here, there is another who keeps to the gardens and lives in a small cottage near the castle. She is more a wise woman and healer to the children and Aine." Rory swiftly reclaimed his blade. In a hushed tone, he added, "Aine is twenty-two summers. When she turned eighteen, those who visited here requested a marriage contract."

"Two and twenty," murmured Alex, brushing more moisture away from his face. "Why did she not accept any offer?"

"A question ye must ask her yourself," responded the man gruffly.

Before Alex had a chance to move forward, Rory blocked his path with an outstretched hand. "Are ye considering the lass for…*marriage*?"

Alex took a hesitant step back, shaken by the man's words. "Nae, *nae*," he sputtered and quickly added, "I am too old for her."

A great roar of laughter pealed forth from Rory. Smacking Alex hard on the back, he argued, "By the Gods! Ye do not even ken *your* age, so why concern yourself with hers?"

Alex grumbled a curse and walked away. Striding with intent, he gave a curt nod in passing when Aine stepped from her safe haven.

She hurried after him. "Ye are bleeding."

"Aye," he returned, making long strides through the bailey and ignoring her concern.

"The cut requires tending to. Glenna is a healer. I can take ye there," she suggested, doing her best to keep up with him.

"Nae need."

"What do ye mean?" she pressed.

Alex clenched his jaw. Rory's talk about marriage settled like a nettle's sting. Without a clear path in front of him, he had no intention of luring any woman into his life with false hope. Especially the one who smelled like wildflowers on a spring day, with enchanting eyes that beguiled him.

"The wound will heal in time," he gritted out, sweeping past a yew tree and heading toward the sounds of a nearby stream.

Aine grasped his arm with a force that surprised him. "Can ye stop for a moment!"

Halting his stride, he glared down at her. The look he gave her would singe the hair from any warrior or animal. "Do ye have more to say?"

"Why do ye refuse aid?" she demanded, fisting her hands on her round hips.

Her stubborn refusal to leave intrigued Alex. Would she flee if he challenged her? He lowered his head near hers. "Why do ye care?"

Her eyes widened, and her luscious lips parted. "Because I do," she whispered.

Alex's breathing became shallow and the air around them thick. Her pink lips begged to be kissed. Would they be as sweet as berries? Or as heady as the wine he drank last evening? An ache to take her in his arms filled him.

He wrestled with the conflict—duty, honor, possession. She was pure as new-fallen snow on a crisp morn, and he no better than a rutting stag. Though his hands shook to hold her in his arms, Alex steeled his emotions and moved away from her.

Ye deserve a better man, Aine. Ye are a beauty, and I am but a beast.

Aine's smile came slowly as she took a step toward him and did the unthinkable. Standing on her tiptoes, she brushed a kiss along his bearded cheek. "Is it wrong to care for ye?"

Indecision plagued him as he regarded her— disbelieving, curious as to what his real fear might be. Shoving aside the conflict within, Alex grasped her around the waist. He nuzzled the spot below her ear. "Ye tempt your fate with a kiss, Aine? With a man ye do not ken?"

She lifted her gaze to his—her cheeks flushed with a rosy hue. "Did I tempt ye?"

And there Alex witnessed the invitation in the smoldering depths of her lavender eyes. By the hounds! What was the lass doing? She had transformed to a siren, tempting him beyond reason, luring him with her heady scent and enticing song.

With his restraint failing, Alex deemed a lesson proved in order—one that would hopefully frighten her away from him. His eyes raked boldly over her lush curves. Crushing Aine to his chest, he devoured what she had to offer. The kiss became demanding, urgent, forcing her to open fully to the seduction and pleasure. His tongue quested with a burning need to conquer—

slipping inside her sweetness. He drew forth her moan and answered with one of his own, kissing her more deeply. Gripping her waist firmly, Alex slowly walked her backward until her back hit the rough bark of a tree.

The kiss sang through his veins, igniting a hunger beyond anything he had known. Alex angled his head to take more of her sweet lips and hungrily feasted on something he dared not take.

When Aine nudged against the hard length of his cock, Alex stilled. The savage intensity of their kiss blinded him to all rational thought. His body craved to be inside her warmth—to strip her gown and feel her soft ivory flesh against his skin. Then take her maidenhead up against the tree.

On a groan, Alex broke free from her seductive mouth. Resting his forehead against hers, he struggled to rein in his breathing. Desire hammered through his veins as surely as the sun rose each morn.

"That was exquisite," she whispered—her breath warm against his face, enticing him further.

He choked on his laughter. The lass had not been frightened by his demonstration. His tactic merely inflamed her own desire and his own.

"Aye," he murmured, taking a step back and wiping a hand across his brow. Alarmed by his lack of control, he let out a last shuddering breath and moved aside. "Ye should return to the castle, Aine."

"Why?" she asked softly, coming to stand in front of him.

Alex clenched his hands by his sides and looked beyond her. "Because I desire to be alone. Forgive me for touching ye in such a manner."

"Did ye not enjoy kissing me?" she asked in a

shocked tone.

Enjoy? By the Gods, my body is burning after one kiss!

He refused to glance down at her. If he did, Alex feared he'd sweep her back into his arms, and this time he would not stop until he possessed all of her. Squeezing his eyes shut, he snapped, "Did ye not understand my meaning? Leave me alone!"

When all remained quiet, he risked opening his eyes and found Aine had indeed slipped silently away.

Alex slammed his fist against the ancient tree. Emotions warred inside him—frustration and anger, lust and desire. "When my mind is healed, there will be a day of reckoning with the Gods! 'Tis a cruel fate ye have given me."

Chapter Seven

"Kisses are like wishes. The more ye take, the more ye want." ~Fae Lore

"Men!" spat out Aine as the flames snapped around the hot steel she fashioned within the forge. "Irritating, stubborn, confusing! First Keegan, then Uncle Eamon and Rory!" She twisted the metal surrounded by the fire and sighed heavily. "Now, Alex. Why bother with men at all? They're always telling me what to do—how to feel."

Drawing forth the blade, she placed it on the anvil and began to level the hammer against her latest project, attempting to quell her anger with each blow. "Why did I kiss him? Why did I allow him to kiss me so passionately? I barely ken the man!"

Discouraged with the blade's progression, she tossed the metal into the water and watched the steam hiss into the air. Afterward, Aine placed the dirk back on the anvil and walked away.

For three days, she stayed away from Alex, even taking her meals in her chamber. Believing solitude and hard work would banish the thoughts of the man, she found they merely inflamed her emotions. Visions of their heated encounter slipped into her dreams each night. His face loomed over her, taking claim to her body. Upon waking, her skin rippled with desire—desire to learn what Alex's touch could awaken within her. An ache settled between her thighs, unsettling and confusing her even more.

"Enough. 'Tis foolish to dwell on dreams," she lamented.

Retreating to the back of the forge, Aine leaned against the wooden gate and grimaced. Once again, the goats had escaped and were busy munching on tufts of grass which had managed to escape the harshness of the newly fallen snow.

She snapped her fingers at them. "I am in nae mood to run after ye again. Finish your meal and return home."

They were content on foraging for more food and ignored her outburst.

Aine glared at them. "Too bad I do not have the power like our guest Fae warrior. He would whisk ye away with a single thought."

"Tsk, tsk, Aine. Would ye truly use magic?" scolded Glenna. The woman came striding through the path between the trees, carrying a basket looped over her arm. "Let the animals wander back when they are ready. The cold bite of the north wind will be a warning to return to the warmth of their pen."

"My words were spoken aloud to those who would not berate me. The animals cannot condemn me."

Glenna studied her warily. "If your anger fuels ye to make a rash decision, what will happen beyond this haven? Or when ye encounter those who do not live with magic?"

Aine shrugged. Uncertainty had twisted all her plans the moment she had kissed Alex and then been rejected. "I have abandoned my plans to travel beyond Castle Taloch," she argued, opening the gate to let her friend inside.

"What?" gasped the woman almost dropping her basket.

Steadying her friend, Aine led her to a nearby chair. "Considering recent events, 'tis wiser to remain here."

Fury sparked within Glenna's eyes. Instead of sitting down, she dropped her basket on the chair. "What has happened?"

Aine met her heated stare. "Too many *magical* wishes."

"Has this anything to do with the recent traveler?"

"Nae," she lied and returned to the gate. The crisp air soothed her burning cheeks at the memory of Alex's kiss. Without thought, her fingers brushed against her lips, bringing forth the fire of passion. His taste lingered inside her, even after three days of food and ale.

Glenna approached by her side. "Where is my friend Aine Fraser? The one who spoke of dreams beyond this place. She yearned to experience the land of Scotland— to seek and belong with others who shared her lineage." Her friend's voice took a more somber tone. "I recall a woman intent on forging her destiny—strong, aye, stubborn, but one who reached for the stars for a possible future."

Swallowing the lump of bitterness, Aine shook her head. "The reality of truth hit *your friend* firmly in the heart. I am nae a young lass, dreaming of tales. Certainly, I possess and favor more of my father's traits than my mother's."

"So ye chain yourself to this life to use *magic*?" chastised Glenna and jabbed her in the arm.

Rubbing her fingers across her forehead, Aine tried to ease the pain seeping in behind her eyes. "'Tis for the best."

"Ye are not telling me everything, are ye?"

Some secrets are best kept buried. Aine tucked a stray lock of hair behind her ears. "I grow weary of this conversation. Can ye share why ye are here?"

Glenna sighed and gestured toward the basket. "Eamon sent a message stating the new traveler required healing aid. I have come with herbs, balms, and bandages."

Aine snorted. "Aye. He suffered a wound from his time in the lists with Rory. I did try and persuade him to seek ye out for healing, though he *stubbornly* refused."

"The Fae warrior is here?" The woman went to retrieve her basket. "Why has nae one summoned me? Did he bring back any news from the Fae realm? Or maybe fresh herbs from the Master Apothecary?"

A smile twitched on Aine's mouth. Unlike the others who lived within the castle and became giddy with excitement when visitors arrived from the Fae realm, Glenna usually resonated a calmness. However, she found this sudden new demeanor in her friend a pleasant surprise to witness.

Aine removed her working smock and tossed it over the chair. Gently brushing out the folds in her gown, she tried to smooth the wrinkles. "Rory has an interest in the traveler and will remain here until his mind heals."

"By the Goddess, what was the Fae warrior thinking by hitting the man so hard? Eamon stated Keegan had done the same when the man entered our forest."

Laughter bubbled forth from Aine. "'Tis not what ye believe." Reaching for her cloak off a peg by the gate, Aine wrapped the garment around her shoulders. "Walk with me, and I shall tell ye what has occurred. The traveler's name is Alex. Furthermore, Rory kens the man. In truth, I think the man's head is made of stone."

Glenna retrieved her basket and looped an arm through Aine's. "Ye must tell me all before we reach the great hall."

While they strolled together out of the forge, Aine divulged everything she knew about Alex MacFhearguis to her friend. Thankfully, Glenna kept her questions to herself—nodding every so often. When Aine finished giving her account, she held her breath, fearing the woman would seek more answers to her questions.

"Often, the Goddess guides those into our world for *her* purpose," mused Glenna. She paused and gently cupped a hand against Aine's cheek. "Do not embrace the bitterness simply because ye have encountered a huge boulder along your journey. Either find a way around or accept those who have put this man in your path."

Confusion swirled like a tempest within Aine. "Now ye are comparing a man to a boulder?"

Glenna relinquished her hold on Aine's arm and waved to a passing lad. "Are they not the same? Unmoving and as thick as steel?"

Before Aine could respond, Rory steadily made his way toward them.

"Glenna," greeted Rory with an outstretched hand for them to proceed him into the castle. "Are ye here to tend to our new visitor?"

The woman nodded. "Aye. Curious why ye have taken to sparring with humans, but then, Aine has spoken how ye ken the man. Can ye share more?"

"As I have stated to Eamon and Aine, I cannot give ye any more knowledge. We must all wait for Alex to regain his memories. On his own without the aid of telling him details of his life."

Content to follow silently behind them, Aine paused by the entrance of the great hall. Her breathing hitched. Alex stood gazing into the blazing hearth. Firelight danced off his rugged profile, and she stood mesmerized. All the anguish from the past few days vanished with one look. The man was all hard lines and strength, from his chiseled jaw and broad chest to his thighs. Alex commanded a fierce presence, even more than the Fae warrior striding the expanse of the hall with Glenna.

When Alex lifted his head, his gaze drifted beyond those who greeted him and directly landed on Aine. Uncertainty filled those beautiful eyes, and then instantly his expression hardened.

Her body trembled, unable to move forward. Recalling his earlier words to leave him alone, Aine turned to leave.

"Come join us." Rory beckoned to her.

She shook her head. "Goats need to be gathered and returned to their pen."

"Do ye have need of my assistance, *again*?" asked Alex. The low timbre of his voice sent a tingling sensation over her skin.

Aine started to stammer a denial, but her words tangled like knots on a loom when she glanced over her shoulder at the man. Amusement flickered in the eyes that met hers, and she fought the smile threatening to steal forth from her lips.

"Ye are not going anywhere until I have examined your wound," protested Glenna, pulling out a chair for Alex and motioning him over to her.

"The healer is correct," urged Aine, taking hesitant

steps inside the hall. "Ye do not want to be a victim of a fever sickness."

Without uttering a complaint, Alex took the offered seat, surprising Aine. Steeling her emotions, she clasped her hands together and remained rooted at the opposite end of the table.

While Glenna inspected the ugly wound above his brow, she probed him with questions about pain in his head or limbs. Alex's responses were short and clipped as if he did not like to be fretted over.

The tension which had earlier filled her body lessened with the arrival of the joyous sounds of the children, followed by Uncle Eamon and Etain.

Hamish bounded over toward the men, intent on watching Glenna work her healing skills.

Cara grasped Aine's hand. "I have good news," confessed the young girl.

"Do tell," encouraged Aine.

The lass yanked on her hand. "Ye must bend down."

Aine's eyes widened. "An important secret, aye?"

Giving her a stern look, Cara tugged harder. "Let me tell ye first before Hamish blurts out the news. Ye ken he can never stay silent."

Aine complied and bent down on one knee. "Should I guess?" she teased.

Cupping a hand against the side of Aine's ear, the lass whispered, "We are going to ask the traveler to stay for our midwinter feast, even if his mind heals."

Aine drew back and gaped at her in disbelief.

Her reaction seemed to amuse Cara, and she giggled. "Ye have *forgotten* about the feast."

"Sweet Goddess, aye," muttered Aine. She had nae worries about Alex. Nae, her concern now settled elsewhere. "When is midwinter?"

"Twelve days."

Squeezing the girl's hand, Aine whispered, "I pray ye have not given me a chore in the kitchens."

"Only chopping. Rowena does not trust ye with anything else." Cara released her hand. "She says ye can do nae harm with the vegetables."

"Good to hear Rowena has trust in my knife skills," Aine responded dryly and stood.

Cara clapped her hands. Dashing over to her brother, she twitched back and forth on her toes, waiting for Glenna to finish with Alex. As soon as the healer pronounced all remained well with the man, Cara stepped forward.

Placing her small hand on Alex's arm, she beamed up at him. "Sir, we would be honored to have ye share our feast at midwinter."

"'Tis almost midwinter?" The warmth of his smile echoed in his voice.

The young girl bobbed her head in acknowledgement.

"Will there be much food and drink?"

"Oh, aye," confirmed Cara, adding, "And Aine will bring her harp and sing for us."

"I will?" squeaked Aine, hesitant to perform in front of the man.

Cara swept her a sly smile. "Aye. Ye have a lovely voice and sing beautiful songs."

Alex's smile widened in approval. "Then I look forward to the feasting."

Squirming under his gaze, Aine leaned against the table for support. Did something happen to the man after three full days? He actually looked pleased to be around her.

"Let me warn ye, the hall can get extremely boisterous," interjected Eamon while pouring a cup of ale.

Hamish laughed. "Like the time one of the Dragon Knights danced on the long table, jumping over the swords?"

A hushed silence descended like storm clouds within the hall.

Alex stood slowly. His good humor stilled, and his countenance grew serious. With each rise and fall of his breath, he appeared to struggle with his thoughts. Shifting his stance, he fisted his hands on his hips.

"Are ye unwell?" asked Glenna.

Alex ignored the woman's question. Turning his attention to Rory, he glared at him. "Angus MacKay is the leader of the *Dragon Knights*?"

"Aye," Rory confirmed slowly.

He remembers! Aine held her breath, waiting for the man to finally share more.

Alex stiffened, his eyes narrowing at the Fae. "Ye are not a Dragon Knight, but I do ken ye from somewhere."

Rory rubbed a hand over his chin. "We do ken each other, but I cannot force the memory from ye."

"Lugh's balls!" growled Alex, stepping toward the man. "Then ye must be my enemy, if ye have nae wish to aid me. Is my name truly Alex?"

Aine glanced sharply at Glenna and pointed to Cara and Hamish, praying she would understand her meaning.

The woman gave her a sharp nod and grasped the hands of the children, escorting them out of the great hall. Their protests echoed along the entryway, with

Etain lumbering after the group.

Rory dared to place a firm hand on Alex's shoulder. "I can assure ye, I am not your enemy, and aye, 'tis your name."

Alex shoved him aside. "Then explain why ye cannot tell me who I am? If not, I am leaving this wretched place."

Aine twisted her fingers within the folds of her gown. *This is all my fault. The man does not comprehend what has been done to him. How can we help him to understand, Goddess? Am I not responsible for my own actions? Is this not what we have learned here? To be brave and face our greatest fears?*

Laughter threatened to burst forth from her at the sudden revelation.

Drawing in a deep breath, Aine exhaled softly and pushed away from the table. Striding with intent toward the two men, she disregarded the warning look her uncle gave her and shook her head at him in dismissal. Determined to right a wrong, Aine went to Alex's side.

Reaching for his hand, a small smile of apprehension touched her lips. "I can share some knowledge with ye, since I caused ye to venture through the forest."

"*Aine*," warned Rory.

She lifted her chin and defied the elder. "'Tis my story to tell. 'Tis my fault what has befallen the man. Would ye wish him harm by allowing him to leave and cross through the forest alone?"

Rory's jaw clenched. But he finally relented and dipped a slight bow. "Again, be careful what ye have wished for, Aine." The elder turned from her. "Eamon, we have a roof to inspect."

Her uncle garbled a response of protest but swiftly complied and followed Rory out of the hall.

Alex's guarded look eased slightly. Returning to the table, he motioned for her to join him. "Give me your account."

"I would prefer to stand." She gave him a small smile, hoping to persuade the man. If his fury came to another boil, she'd bolt from the hall.

Alex braced his hands on the table. "Do not make me ask again, Aine. I am weary of the secrets, and apparently ye contain the key. Now please sit down."

With reluctance, Aine settled into the chair. "Would ye like some ale?"

The man smirked. "Nae." Dragging another chair from by her side, he sat across from her.

"Even if ye left, ye would not be able to find your way home," she began.

Alex leaned back and folded his arms across his chest. "Continue."

Aine swallowed with difficulty and found her voice. "Ye came through the veiled mists into a special forest. A haven for those who are learning wisdom without the benefit of...*magic*. I am sorry, but 'tis I who parted the mists and brought ye on through. Until my uncle and Rory can determine how to undo the magic, ye are trapped in this realm."

His brows drew together in an agonized expression, and he stood abruptly, causing the chair to topple back onto the floor. Shock quickly yielded to fury.

She started to speak, but he silenced her with a slash of his hand.

Reaching for a jug of ale, Alex poured a heavy amount into a cup. He drained the contents in two large swallows, and then refilled his cup. Wiping his mouth with the back of his hand, he then went to the blazing hearth.

His bitter laughter surrounded Aine. But his words sent a chill of unease down her spine.

"Say nae more. Ye and the others are *Fae*," he spat out in disgust. "And Rory MacGregor is a Fenian warrior."

Chapter Eight

"Never assume a Fae warrior is your ally."
~MacFhearguis Motto

Keenly aware of Aine's scrutiny, Alex kept his back turned and his distance from her. He stared into the flames snapping within the hearth, attempting to sort out the swirling images within his mind. One after the other, they tumbled through his thoughts. His gut clenched, recalling battles, Fae warriors, deaths, and the path which led him into the forest after a heated conversation with his brother over another midwinter feast.

Fear and anger twisted inside him. *I am trapped with the Fae!* Curses flew from his mouth at the revelation.

He downed the remaining ale and flung the empty cup into the fire. He required something stronger to take away the fury coursing through his veins—like the amber liquid he once enjoyed at the castle of the Dragon Knights. Pinching the bridge of his nose, Alex fought for control.

"I ken ye are angry—"

"*Angry?*" he replied in reckless rage and stormed to her side. Alex pounded his chest with his fist. "I have *nae* fondness for the Fae. They go to any gains to manipulate a man's fate. Meddling, irritating, rude, dominating, *and* content to rule their power over us."

She flinched but made no move to depart. "Ye have

all your memories?"

Alex hesitated, measuring her for a moment. "Aye! My name is Alex MacFhearguis, and I am the chieftain of Leòmhann Castle. Though I am certain ye ken these details about my life."

Rising from her chair, she glared at him with burning, reproachful eyes. "Unfortunately, *Elder Rory* did not share this wisdom about ye, only your name. He withheld any knowledge to let your mind heal on its own. And I have offered my earnest regrets for what has occurred."

Frustration seethed within him. Questions he wanted to toss out at her became wedged on his tongue. He raked a hand through his hair. "Why in the Gods' name did ye part the veil?"

Aine stiffened. He noted the conflict over her features. "I sought out another to take me to your Scotland," she responded in a low, tormented voice. Lowering her head, she continued, "I reckoned the time had come for me to venture onward with the help of a traveler. My intentions spoken from my heart went wrong. I should have waited until we received a message from the Fae elders. Uncle Eamon is the only one permitted to part the veil."

Alex sighed heavily. He had directed his anger at her, instead of the fates for bringing him here, and at a certain Fae warrior.

He tipped up her chin with his finger, forcing her to meet his concerned gaze. "Ye are safer here. The new religion sweeping *my Scotland* makes dwelling there unsafe for ye and your kind."

A rosy stain spread across her cheeks and the bridge of her nose. Alex fought the temptation to trail his fingers over her smooth skin.

"Half of my blood flows with Scotland—from my mother," she confessed, tersely. "And your words are full of untruths about the Fae. We are kind, gentle, strong, generous, and loving. Most of us have spent our entire life managing to do without magic, so one day we can return and live among other people. Ye might have harsh words for the Fenian warrior, but ye ken *nothing* about us. And I, for one, do not fear the new religion. Uncle Eamon has counseled us, and once, a monk traveled through our forest."

Her confession startled Alex. "The Fae side is from your father? Where are your kin now?" Dropping his hand, his words came out more harsh than he intended.

"My father is dead," she replied solemnly. "I do not ken what has befallen my mother after she departed the castle. Keegan has more memories of her than me. In truth, I am relieved I cannot recall her. I was told her time here left her unsettled—she battled between staying and leaving. When she pleaded with my father to return to her village, alone, he granted her request. She was not strong enough to raise two children and show them how not to use their magic."

Aine turned her head away from his censure. "We were born outside Taloch. With our powers growing at an early age, he thought bringing us here to live would help her understand our magic, but she hated being separated from the Scotland she knew. And she grew to despise our Fae wisdom." Her shoulders sagged. "My father never spoke of her again after she departed, and a part of his soul died the day she slipped through the veil."

A heaviness centered in Alex's chest. He lashed out and brought sorrow to the one person who radiated joy—

Aine. First, by kissing her, followed by his rejection. Then he subjected the lass to his fury. Alex yearned to take her into his arms and soothe the hurt and confusion. He struggled with words to ease her sorrow.

"Nae mother should leave their bairns, unless death claims them," he uttered softly.

A tear rolled down her cheek. "My uncle spoke those exact words after she left us."

Unable to stop himself, Alex cupped her face in his hands. Brushing away the moisture with the pad of his thumb, he said, "Forgive me for my bitterness." He felt himself drowning in a meadow of lavender fields as she stared up at him.

"Did ye not speak from your *heart*, Alex MacFhearguis?"

He chuckled and wiped away a smudge of grime from her nose. "Aye, *aye*, but they should have been directed toward *another* Fae."

She batted his hand away in obvious embarrassment. "Rory did warn me that ye would be angry once your memories returned."

Alex grimaced in good humor. Releasing his hold, he went to the table and poured ale into two cups. Returning to her side, he offered one to her and proposed, "Let us start anew, Aine Fraser. 'Tis a fine home ye have here."

Her fingers brushed against his when she accepted the cup. Aine gave him a smile that sent his blood racing. "Welcome to Castle Taloch, Alex MacFhearguis. I am eager to hear about Leòmhann and your kin." She paused and regarded him over the rim of her cup. "Or wife?"

Sputtering on the ale, Alex shook his head. "Nae, *nae wife*," he managed.

She took a sip of her ale and wandered over to an alcove, settling onto the cushioned seat.

Alex followed and leaned against the stone enclosure. "What exactly is this haven I have heard others discussing?"

Aine shifted her position. "The castle and surrounding lands offer us a *haven* from the outside world. Whenever a traveler arrives, the man or woman is greeted with respect due any new guest. Usually, the person is for someone dwelling here—either for a child or someone older. And there are times when the visitor is simply passing through. The Fae have permitted these guests to venture through our land on whatever journey they are seeking. We never question the reasoning."

More Fae interference. "Why are there so many children living here?"

Pursing her lips, she lowered her head and glanced away.

The silence lengthened between them, making Alex uncomfortable. "If ye rather not speak of them, I shall say nae more."

After taking another sip of her ale, Aine gestured for him to take a seat beside her.

"Not enough room, unless ye desire to sit on my lap."

Laughter as sweet as bells burst forth from the woman. "And risk having another see us? Nae. And 'tis difficult staring up at a giant."

Alex arched a brow. *'Tis time I make amends to ye.* "I have nae regrets for kissing ye. Only for my harsh words afterward. Furthermore, the doors to the hall are closed, and I'll refrain from kissing ye."

Her hand shook as she finished the ale in her cup.

A frown marred her forehead when he removed the cup from her hand. After he deposited both cups on the floor, Alex picked up Aine into his arms and settled her onto his lap.

"What are ye doing?" she rasped out, placing her palms against his chest.

His gaze fell to the creamy expanse of her neck. "Waiting for ye to explain."

"Can ye not go back to standing?" she demanded, moving her hands around his neck.

"Why?" he argued.

Aine's tongue darted out along her lower lip, and her hands tightened around him.

By the Gods, how she inflamed his desires. Never had he wanted another woman as much as the one seated within his arms. She broke away the steel gates inside his heart—warming a void he allowed no one to enter.

"Is this truly what ye want, Aine—for me to stand?" He breathed the words against her soft skin. "If so, release *your* hold on me."

She yanked on his hair, forcing him to meet her gaze. "I cannot think with ye so close. There, I've confessed my reason. Now if ye insist on cradling me like a bairn on your lap, I guess I shall have to quickly answer your question."

Chuckling softly, Alex nodded.

Aine's fingers loosened, and excitement flared within Alex. She chose not to remove her hands from around his neck, and this pleased him. With steely control, he waited patiently for her to speak.

Her voice carried a distant tone when she began, "We are children of Fae and human—neither welcomed in the realm of the Fae, nor accepted with magical gifts in your world. Many of us have been abandoned and left to forge for ourselves. Or worse, die among the harsh elements. Eons ago, the King of the Fae found out what his own people had done. What they had created. After the edict had been proclaimed, Guardians were appointed across Scotland and Ireland to protect these abandoned half-Fae children. Either we learn the ways of our human half or remain forever in the safe shelter with our Guardian."

"And Uncle Eamon is your Guardian," interjected Alex, trying to hide his displeasure over the miserable Fae and humans who brought such dishonor upon their family.

"Aye, and brother to our father. We are fortunate to have him as kin."

Tugging on one of her stray curls, he pressed, "So my arrival into this realm was not planned?"

Her troubled gaze met his. "Nae, Alex. My magic drew ye into this world."

Worry infused his next question, fearing her reply. "And nae one can send me back? Not even Rory?"

She scowled and lowered her arms. "Rory is consulting with elders in the Fae council."

Alex felt the loss of her hands around him keenly. "I need Rory to get a message to my brother. I have been away far too long."

Aine cupped a hand over her mouth in obvious mirth.

"Ye find humor in worrying my kin?" His tone laced with scorn.

"Goodness, nae," she soothed, placing her warm palm against his cheek. "Ye must understand time moves differently between your world and mine."

"Regardless, I must get a message to my brother, Patrick."

Her eyes widened. "How?"

"A certain Fenian warrior can get a message to the MacFhearguis clan," he explained, not wanting to remove her from the comforts of his arms.

Aine winced and started twisting the ties on his tunic. "There might be a problem."

He let out a growl of displeasure. "Explain."

"As I stated earlier, Rory is consulting with the Fae—"

Alex gripped her hands. "Are ye telling me Rory has left the castle? Gone?"

"Aye," she confirmed.

"Do ye ken when he will return?"

She lifted a shoulder. "Rory expressed this meeting might take time."

"Bloody, annoying Fae! Could he not have waited?" Alex noted her raised brow, and responded, "Do not answer the question. Between Fae warriors and Dragon Knights, I reckon this shall be a long midwinter."

Aine disarmed all his fury with her charming smile. "Ye do ken the MacKay clan, also known as the Dragon Knights, are part Fae?"

"Also, for a time, our sworn enemy," added Alex, releasing her hands.

She tapped a finger against those lips he craved. "We did hear the news about the great battle, along with an alliance forming between your clan and the Dragon Knights. They carry the blood of the Fae upon their creation hundreds of years ago."

Alex brushed a hand down the back of his neck. "I have heard the tale spouted by my grandsire and *numerous* bards."

"Will ye truly be displeased staying here for a time until Rory and Uncle Eamon can find a way to return ye to Leòmhann?"

His expression softened. Unsure how to respond, Alex resigned to another fate presented to him and wrestled with the conflict.

I should not be here. I should not like ye. I should not want ye.

But the truth slammed into Alex with a force that stole the breath from his lungs. He found the enchanting Fae lass mesmerizing—from the grime of the smithy on her face to the shimmer within her eyes. Although his desire to bed the lass consumed him, there happened to be another feeling woven in his thoughts. He yearned more from Aine than a simple bedding. The lass intrigued him.

And this frightened Alex. He'd never permitted any woman to invade the emptiness inside his heart. Alex deemed the emotion of love a weakness. Even though his brothers had found solace with their wives, he considered taking a wife merely to produce an heir.

Why do I care if I have sons? Patrick and Adam have already ensured the lineage of the MacFhearguis clan with their offspring.

"Ye are *thinking* too much," she murmured, smoothing the hair back from his forehead.

"Plagued with indecision," he choked out, tucking her small hand into his.

Aine frowned, struggling to remove herself from his lap. "I shall leave ye with your displeasure and indecisions."

"Nae!" he ordered, gripping her shoulders. Alex

struggled to find the words to explain. With a heavy sigh, he slammed the door on his troubling thoughts and acted on his emotions. Brushing a gentle kiss on her forehead, he relived the velvet warmth of her mouth with their first kiss.

"Kiss me again," she urged, slipping her arms once again around his neck.

Alex required no further invitation.

His lips seared a path down her neck, inhaling her scent. When he lifted his head, Alex kissed her with a hunger that belied his outward calm—feasting on the soft fullness of her lips. The blood hammered in his veins, and his cock strained against his trews, aching to sink deep within her womanly folds. He kissed her with reckless abandon, thrusting his tongue into the soft heat of her mouth. She dueled a passion with her own, which increased his fiery desire to conquer the woman.

Aine squirmed within his arms. "*More*," she pleaded.

Slowly, he eased his hand up the side of her waist until he reached his prize. Placing his palm over her full breast, Alex fondled her, and then pinched the pert nipple through the fabric of her gown.

She wrenched her mouth from his. "Sweet Goddess." Burying her head into his neck, she traced her tongue along the vein. "My body burns for ye, Alex."

On a guttural groan, Alex drew Aine away from him. *What am I doing? And in the great hall?*

His voice shook with need. "Nae more kisses."

She frowned in obvious confusion. "Why?"

After removing her from his lap, Alex abruptly stood and raked a hand through his hair. "Because kissing ye will not be enough."

Aine took a step toward him. Her smile came slowly. "I ken what happens between a man and a woman."

Alex found himself shaking and clenched his hands. *By the hounds, ye are a siren.* "This is not a game," he growled. Reaching for her hand, he placed it over his cock. "My need is fierce."

She bit her lower lip but made no attempt to free her hand. "And what about mine?" she challenged.

Never in all his life had Alex met a woman so headstrong and stirring. Yet he had never kissed one who was part Fae. Did she weave words of enchantment through him? He banished the thought.

Beads of sweat broke out along his brow. Alex stole a glance at the closed doors. Returning his attention to the beauty in front of him, he leaned near her ear. "Would ye wish to give up your maidenhead to someone who will eventually leave here?"

Slipping her hand free, Aine's expression sobered. "Perchance ye will not please me. Therefore, I shall not dread our parting."

Ye are lying, lass. Fear reflects in your eyes.

Alex wrapped an arm around her waist and pinned her with his gaze as well. Unable to hold back the words, they poured forth like the river rushing toward the seas. "Trust me, Aine, after I have bedded ye, there will be nae others. Your body shall ken pleasures unlike any ye have known. I intend to take ye to the stars when I claim your body."

With great effort, Alex drew Aine away from him and turned her toward the doors of the great hall. Grasping her hips from behind, he brushed one final kiss along the soft spot below her ear and murmured, "The next time I take a kiss from ye, your body shall be mine."

Aine trembled beneath his touch before dashing from the hall.

Chapter Nine

"Once you've plucked the harp strings of love, ye are forever in its embrace." ~Fae Lore

After securing the satchel of food to the back of her horse, Aine fastened her cloak firmly around her body. Snow blew inside the stable in soft flakes, dusting the rough wooden floor. "Have ye made friends with Beast?" she inquired softly, smoothing her hand over the glossy mane of her horse.

Drust regarded her, and then blinked. Tossing his head back and forth, he let out a snort.

Aine smirked. "Are ye certain ye have tried? Perchance he grows restless confined to the stables. Is he one to require a daily outing, regardless of the weather?"

She observed the other horse, noting his quiet demeanor. *Ye are similar to your master. He prefers to study and remain quiet.*

Snatching an apple from the sack on the floor, she wandered to the stall where Beast kept silent watching her movements. After removing her small *sgian dubh* from her belt, she sliced the apple into several quarters. She held the pieces outward to the animal. "What is your account on this chilled morn?"

Beast snorted fully—his spittle covering her hand and a part of her cloak.

Her eyes widened in alarm. "'Tis truth? Ye have not

ventured outside the castle? Not even with one of the stable lads?"

The animal pounded the straw-littered ground with his hoof. Then he lowered his head and feasted on the offering she presented.

"Have ye made another friend?" asked Keegan, entering the warmth of the stables and shutting the door behind him.

"Aye," she confirmed, stroking her fingers down the animal's nose. "From the first moment I spoke to him." Glancing sharply at her brother, she added, "Though Beast refused to give me details of his life with Alex *or* his surname."

Keegan folded his arms over his chest and lounged casually against a wooden post. "The beast refused to acknowledge me or Hamish. Even Cara is unable to charm the animal. Ye are the only one who has made a connection."

Aine looked away from her brother's questioning stare. "Ye ken 'tis my gift to speak with the animals, so why are ye concerned?"

"And Cara?" he pressed, ignoring her question.

She continued to stroke the horse's muzzle. "Her gift is far greater with the land and with visions."

"The animals do speak with her," corrected Keegan. "But this horse remained silent with the lass. Interesting…"

She glanced sideways at him. "Perchance Cara is learning to hone her gifts with the land and chooses not to converse with the animals. She is also preparing herself for the day when a Seer is required, either here or in Scotland."

"Horse dung!" spat out Keegan, plucking a straw

loose from a pile of hay.

Irritated over his bitterness and the conversation, Aine turned to face her brother. "Is there a matter ye wish to discuss with me? Or do ye find my friendship with the horse irritating because he belongs to Alex?"

Keegan discarded the piece of hay. "The man is not worthy of ye."

"Wh...*what* are ye saying?" stammered Aine, clenching her fists by her side.

"Alex observes ye as prey—like a hawk. Hungry for the hunt and feast." Keegan loomed over her.

She blinked in confusion. Then her anger surfaced like a tempest. Jabbing a finger into his chest, Aine spat out, "How dare ye! I am not a feeble bird to be harvested and eaten. I am a woman. Furthermore, Alex is a chieftain! Rory mentioned the man is honorable."

Keegan snarled. "So *honorable* that he craves to have ye in his bed?"

Aine let out a gasp.

Her brother's triumphant sneer at unraveling the truth meant only one thing to her. He had prodded the mind of their guest using magic.

Unable to stop herself, she slapped her brother across the face. Her fury and anguish so great, her breathing became labored. Placing a palm against her chest, Aine tried to still the fierce beating of her heart. Slowly regaining her composure, she then took a shaky step back.

Hurt swelled uncomfortably and lodged like a stone in her throat. When she responded, her voice remained tight with strain. "Ye have brought dishonor to yourself, Keegan. Whatever lurks within the mind of Alex MacFhearguis is not for ye to discover. As a member of

Castle Taloch, ye have broken a severe edict—one that saddens me."

His brow furrowed. "Ye ken *nothing* about the ways of men, Aine," he explained, reaching out to her. "Can ye be obedient in their world? Do ye honestly reckon any man would permit ye to work in a forge?"

"Nae! Do not come near me." She stiffened. As tears welled within her eyes, Aine found the strength to keep them from spilling down her cheeks. Steeling her emotions, she glared upward at her brother. "Sadly, ye ken nothing about me, Keegan. Nothing about my needs, wants, desires. When the time comes for Alex to depart, I pray the Goddess allows me to go with him."

Her brother started to protest another complaint, but Aine held her palm outward to halt his words. "Do not interfere. Do not tell me what to do with my life, ever again. What awaits me on the other side is for me to learn. Do ye understand, Keegan? Give me your vow—this day, this moment to never look into the mind of anyone else, including Alex. Or ye force me to go to Uncle Eamon *and* Elder Rory."

A look of fear passed briefly within his eyes. "To have them bind my powers?"

"Worse," she uttered with conviction. "They would strip ye of all powers and banish ye from this haven. Forever."

"Ye would betray me? Your kin?"

"Yet ye have betrayed me, Keegan. Ye do not trust me to make my own decisions."

"I swore to Father to protect and defend ye, and I ken the law," he protested, moving toward the stable doors.

"Then why take a risk by breaking an ancient edict?"

she demanded. "Did ye honestly believe I'd remain silent and do your bidding my entire life? Stay enclosed in this world that can give me nothing in return? Aye, I am willful, stubborn, and do not abide by the rules women follow outside of this realm. But 'tis my decision, not yours, Keegan. As for your vow to our father, ye overstep certain boundaries. Often, Father scolded ye when ye became over protective."

Keegan's features softened. He peered over his shoulder at her. "What if the man hurts ye, Aine? What if he takes but does not give in return? Consider what happened to our parents."

"Our parents made their own fate. Alas, they did not have a happy life. Yet *we* can carve our own destinies and not be chained by the blood of our parents," she returned.

A thin line of displeasure formed on his mouth as he turned to depart.

"Your vow to me," reminded Aine.

Her brother kept his back to her, but she heard his reply as if he had seared the words into her mind. "I swear by the ancient Gods and Goddesses I will not look into the mind of another."

"Keegan?"

"Aye?"

"Ye have bound your oath to me. Be wary of the strength of your gifts. One day, ye might find these powers to be your undoing. Either learn to harness them or accept ye cannot leave Taloch."

Her brother made no attempt to respond.

Aine watched as he slipped out of the stables. Her legs trembled as she struggled to move to a bench. Collapsing onto the rough wood, she closed her eyes and rubbed her temples with her fingers. The intensity of his powers grew with each passing year, and Keegan appeared content not to control them.

In their heated conversation, she dared not express her own feelings to be with Alex. Then Aine pondered if her brother had slipped into her thoughts.

"Nae," she muttered. "Surely I'd have felt your sting of disapproval."

"Are ye unwell?" asked a familiar male voice. The timbre of his question wrapped her in a blanket of warmth.

Aine opened her eyes and raised her head. Alex's large form blocked what small light seeped into the stables. Flakes of snow swirled around the man as if he commanded the elements. Her mouth became dry. *Would ye hurt my heart, Alex?* Swiftly banishing the unwelcome thought, Aine stood.

"Nae. Simply a misunderstanding with my brother." Aine went to her horse's stall. "I thought to visit Glenna to collect herbs and greenery for the midwinter feast. Would ye like to escort me?"

The man studied her for a moment. "Snow is falling."

"Her home is not far. Are ye afraid of a few cold flakes?"

Alex roared with laughter—rich and warm. "Are *ye* not afraid of anything, *leannán*?"

Aine's hand froze on the stall's gate. His term of endearment for her caused her heart to beat wildly. *Until I met ye, nae, Alex.*

Composing her features, she gestured to her horse. "Let me introduce ye to Drust. A gift given to me on my eighteenth summer from the Prince of the Fae's wife,

Ivy."

"Conn MacRoich—prince and leader of the Fenian Warriors," he commented, walking past her, and tending to his own horse. "I am curious why Ivy would part with her horse."

Leading Drust from his stall, she explained, "Princess Ivy realized I favored the animal when I visited her home. In truth, the princess considered the gift a wise decision."

When all remained quiet, Aine stole a glance around her horse.

Alex gaped at her. "Ye have been in the Fae realm?"

"Aye," she confirmed, reaching for her leather gloves from the bench. "Upon our eighteenth year, we are allowed to enter into our other homeland and stay for nine days. 'Tis a time of celebration, feasts, and gifts. Although we are not permitted to live there, we are treated with respect until we return to this world."

An impatient Beast nudged the back of Alex with his muzzle. He turned and gave the animal a stern look of warning.

She giggled. "Beast is anxious to stretch his legs. I deem he grows weary of being trotted around the bailey."

Giving the animal a firm pat on his side, he opened the stall door. "My apologies, my friend. Now that my mind has healed, though my brother, Patrick, would disagree, I'll attend to my duties and oversee your care."

"Is your brother a good man?" inquired Aine. After putting on her gloves, she led her horse out of the stables.

Alex followed behind her. "He is. Are ye certain time moves differently here?"

Swiftly mounting her animal, Aine pulled the hood of her cloak over her head and reached for the reins.

"Indeed." Her breath frosted in the chilled air.

Alex grabbed the reins and mounted his horse. He then gave one final pat over Beast's mane. "If this is a haven where ye learn to harness your powers, I suggest ye begin living as if ye are in *my* Scotland," he suggested.

"Truly? For what purpose?" Aine nudged her horse onward.

"The men and lads should learn to guard the tower. A portcullis needs to be built to secure the gate. Protecting the clan is vital to the care of its people. Banish all skills involving magic. Determine the strength and skills from every man, woman, and child. Encourage and build trust as they learn to expand their knowledge. Therefore, they shall be prepared once they leave this shelter."

While they trotted along through the courtyard and over the bridge, Aine listened in rapt attention to Alex's ideas for Castle Taloch. Although there was no threat of danger to them or the castle, the man posed valid concerns. They lived in this protective shield within Scotland. If they were truly to survive in Alex's world, they needed to merge the two.

After leaving the castle, the land opened up before them. Relishing the beauty of their surroundings, Aine let Drust set the pace.

Sunlight burst through the gray light, dancing off the snow-covered path. A hawk drifted overhead in a lazy path. Lifting her head, Aine shielded her eyes and watched the bird's flight. She fought the temptation to reach out in greeting to the bird within its mind. Alex was correct. If she hoped to survive in a harsher Scotland, she'd have to quell the urge to use her power.

But another troubling thought occurred to her.

Bringing her horse to a halt, Aine continued to gaze upward.

Alex approached near her side. "Are ye speaking with the bird?"

Embarrassed by his question, she bit her lower lip. "Usually, I greet all within the animal kingdom, but your words of restraint halted my thoughts to the hawk. As ye might have guessed, my gift is being able to speak with the animals—inside their own minds."

Tilting his head to the side, he confirmed, "Ye are correct."

She drew in a shaky breath and released it slowly. "Speaking with them poses nae threat here or outside this realm. I have learned to be prudent, preferring to have my discussions in private. There is however another troublesome trait I fear may not be welcomed in *your* Scotland."

"Do tell," he encouraged.

"How can I be accepted when I ken nothing about cooking, sewing, or any abilities required by a woman? I tend to the animals and spend my time in a forge crafting blades and brooches. I worry I would not be accepted—fearing the cruelty of Scotland's people."

Alex reached across and snatched her gloved hand into his. His amber eyes darkened, even in the glare of sunlight and their snowy landscape. He leaned forward. Placing her palm against his chest, he avowed, "Fear can be your shield *or* your blade. Do not fear what others may think. When the time comes for ye to venture out of Taloch, I will be by your side." A smile creased the corners of his mouth. "Did I not consent to have ye fashion a dirk for me? And ye forget, the Dragon Knights and their wives dwell in my Scotland."

Her heart soared with the knowledge. Aine wanted to leap into the man's arms. Alex didn't look at her with scorn over her skills.

Touched by his declaration, she found her tongue twisted, unable to return the gesture with a single word of thanks. With each passing day, her warrior continued to prove how unlike any other man she had encountered before, and Aine found her heart opening to another possibility. One where those strange emotions swirling inside her might be the stirring of something new.

Perchance love.

Chapter Ten

"If ye are handed the sword of leadership, accept the blade without uncertainty." ~*MacFhearguis Motto*

Narrowing his gaze, Alex peered through the thicket of bushes and trees, their limbs heavy with snow. The weak sunlight appeared to be fighting the clouds overhead. He scratched the side of his chin. "Are ye certain this path leads to the home of the healer?"

Aine dismounted from her horse. "And for the second time, aye! We shall lead the horses on through the narrow trail."

He swept her a skeptical glance. "The snow is heavy. There are nae markings to assure us this path is leading us in the right direction."

"Sweet Mother Danu," grumbled Aine. Shaking out her cloak to rid the garment of snow, she waved a hand toward herself. "Remember, half-Fae."

Her lips held a firm pout—a tempting feast for Alex. However, he remained sitting on his horse.

"Why are ye staring at me?" Aine peered down at her cloak. "Aye, I'm covered in wet mud, but soon the warm comforts of Glenna's home shall make all right." Her teeth began to chatter while she stomped her feet to rid more slush from her boots.

An icy blast of wind smacked across Alex's face. Swiftly dismounting, he strode to her side and lifted Aine into his arms.

"Stop!" she protested, squirming to get out of his hold.

"Ye are shaking from the harsh weather. Do ye want to risk becoming ill with a fever?" scolded Alex.

Aine tweaked his nose with her fingers. "Ye are chilled yourself."

He winked at her. "Nae. My body is *verra* warm."

She gaped at him like a forlorn fish, and Alex chuckled softly.

Aine quickly snapped her mouth closed. "The co...*cold* does not bother ye?"

"Not with ye in my arms," confessed Alex.

Her smile came slowly, weaving a charm of beauty around her.

What have ye done to me, Aine? Each time I look into your jeweled eyes, I find myself lost. As if the ground collapsed under me.

"We have already been traveling for an hour on our horses. How much farther?" he asked, tearing his gaze away toward the animals.

"Through the trees," she supplied.

After giving a sharp two-burst whistle to the horses, Alex proceeded forward with the animals plodding behind them. He ducked under one of the branches. A large clump of snow landed on top of him. He shook his head to rid himself of the icy mixture.

The woman in his arms burst out in laughter. "If ye do not put me down, I fear ye will be covered in more snow, along with drenching me."

Content to keep his focus on the narrowing path, he disagreed. "Nae, must keep ye warm."

"Ye have already taken away the chill inside me."

When Alex refused to comply to her demand, more snow covered his head, sliding down the back of his neck. Muttering a curse, he made his way slowly onward. "How far do the lands extend?"

"As far as we wish," clarified Aine. "There are nae boundaries in our world."

"And this veil between my world and yours? Is it nearby?" he asked, trudging through more trees heavy with the recent snowfall.

"South, by the stream. Why do ye ask?"

Alex shifted his warm bundle in his arms. "Trying to determine my journey to ye."

"What were ye doing alone at night? In a forest?" she prodded softly.

After placing her feet gently onto the ground, Alex cupped her chin. "Seeking solitude after another frustrating discussion with my brother."

"Can ye share the details of the discussion?"

Alex brushed his thumb over her bottom lip. "About finding a wife for me."

Her expression grew taut. "Ye had nae wish for a wife?"

"At the time, nae. Battles and betrayal have hardened me. Divided loyalties within my clan and being thrust into a leadership soured me to find a wife. Nevertheless, Patrick warned of a day when our eldest brother might fall victim to the blade of our enemy, making me the chieftain. But I discarded the idea, and the one he spoke of to take a wife."

A shadow of annoyance crossed Aine's face. She took a step aside. "We have arrived at Glenna's home." Without waiting for a reply, she turned and pushed aside another heavy tree limb, disappearing from his sight.

Clenching his hands by his sides, Alex fought the confusion coursing inside him. Her abrupt change in demeanor perplexed him. Aye, he once deemed marriage unacceptable. But now? The idea of a wife grew each day with only one woman in mind. *Aine.*

The thought halted him where he stood. *Would ye truly want a man of thirty-four winters, Aine? I have seen the lust shine in your eyes, so I do not disgust ye. But can our union mean more to ye?*

The horses snorted behind him, and Alex raked a hand through his wet hair. Determined to get them out of the bitter cold, he shoved aside his turmoil.

He ducked, shoving aside the heavy limb and entered a small clearing. Snow circled around a stone and wooden house. Smoke drifted in lazy whisps from the hearth within the dwelling. Alex looked beyond and noted another structure. He grasped the reins of the horses, making his way around the cottage. Arriving at the entrance, he shoved open the two doors. Another horse whinnied in greeting from the back stall.

Heaving a sigh, Alex settled the two horses into nearby stalls, finding food and water already in supply. Afterward, he snatched the satchel off Aine's horse.

Alex retreated out of the structure, heading for Glenna's home. At the entrance, he stomped his boots to get rid of the snow and mud. Before he had a chance to go on through, the door opened, and the woman stood poised in welcome.

"Greetings, Alex." She glanced around him. "Where are your horses?"

"I have placed them inside your stables."

She motioned him inside. "I told ye, Aine. 'Tis a good man who cares for his animals before his own needs."

"Aye, *aye*, ye did, Glenna."

Alex heard a heavy dose of sarcasm in Aine's voice when he stepped into the small house. *Why are ye displeased with me?* He continued to stare at Aine until the door banged closed behind him.

"I have prepared a soup of root vegetables, onions, and wild mushrooms." Glenna removed the satchel from his hand and tugged on his arm. "Let me take your cloak and dry the garment by the fire. Aine, give the man a cup of mead to take the chill from his bones."

Silently, Alex unfastened his cloak, allowing the woman to take the garment from his shoulders.

She crossed to the hearth and placed his cloak over the back of a chair facing the blazing fire. After wiping her hand down her gown, she swept her braid over her shoulder. "Sweet Goddess, Aine! What possessed ye to venture out from Taloch on this snowy day?" She deposited the satchel on a long table strewn with mushrooms.

"I required herbs and greenery for the midwinter feast. Rowena is making special breads, and I have tasked myself to fill the hall with the scents of pine and fruit, all woven together with ribbons." Aine approached near Alex and handed him a cup of mead.

Pointing to the window, Glenna complained, "Can ye not see the snowfall? Ye should have waited."

"In truth," began Alex, "the snows were light when we left Taloch."

"Were they *light* when ye left the comforts of your castle and into a forest?" the woman asked, picking up a large spoon from the table and venturing over to the pot of soup.

Alex took a long swill of mead, relishing the honeyed brew on his tongue. "I cannot recall," he lied, wiping a hand over his mouth.

Aine snorted and settled into a chair by the table.

He sent her a scathing look. *Why do ye mock me?* Perplexed by her abrupt change in mood left him reeling with annoyance.

"'Tis fortunate I can send a message with Mab to Taloch that ye will be staying here until the snow lessens."

"For the ni...*night*?" sputtered Aine. Her eyes widened in alarm, and she glanced around the dwelling. "There's barely enough room for two. Nae. We can manage the journey home."

"I have nae complaint with sleeping with the horses," suggested Alex, growing impatient with both women.

Glenna plopped the spoon into the pot and made her way to the door. "My guests do not bed down with the animals. Unless ye prefer the comforts of straw and horse dung? Ye can sleep by the warm hearth. I have extra blankets and furs. And Aine can share my bed."

Alex grimaced and drained the remainder of his mead.

She grabbed her cloak from a peg on the wall near the door. "Stay or leave. 'Tis your decision, though do so after ye have eaten. Discuss the matter among yourselves. I am going to consult with Mab."

"We welcome your generous offer and will spend the night," announced Alex.

Aine scowled and began to tap her fingers along her thigh.

When the door shut behind the woman, Alex

slammed his cup onto the table. "What troubles ye, Aine?"

"Troubles me?" she challenged, rising from her chair. "Without even consulting my opinion, ye have decided we are staying."

Placing his palms on the rough wood, Alex fought the urge to storm around the table and take her into his arms. "Take a look outside. Even ye would have agreed. And ye ken my meaning. Ever since I shared my conversation with my brother, your words have been filled with bitterness as sharp as an adder's bite."

She fisted her hands on her hips. "Oh, aye, I do recall what ye stated earlier." Her tone dripped with scorn. "The conversation where ye had nae plans on marrying." Lowering her voice, she added with mock severity, "Did ye seek to plunder but not commit?"

The mead soured in Alex's gut. "Commit to what?"

"To anything?" Aine began to pace in front of the hearth.

"Ye speak in riddles!" Pushing away from the table, Alex stalked slowly toward her.

Taking a hesitant step back, Aine pointed a warning finger at him. "Stay away!"

A tremor of unease slipped inside Alex, though he refused to halt his progress. "Either ye explain your words right now, or—"

"What? Kiss me senseless? Therefore making me unable to stop ye from going any farther?" interjected Aine.

Stopping mere inches in front of the lass, Alex drawled, "I thought ye enjoyed my kisses?"

She lifted her chin. "Ye told me the next time ye kissed me, ye would take my body."

"Aye," he confirmed slowly. "I am perplexed by this sudden change in disposition, lass."

After darting a glance at the door, Aine resumed her attention to him. Twisting her hands in the folds of her gown, she shook her head. "'Tis nothing."

An awkward silence hung between them. Alex shifted his stance, worried she'd bolt from the house.

Concerned, he pressed, "Ye appear upset over something, and I would like to understand."

Heaving a frustrated sigh, Aine rubbed a hand over her forehead. She raised her head. "Ye have nae plans to marry, aye?"

Alex swallowed. Why this discussion about marriage? Did Aine desire marriage? To him? He started to reach for her but clenched his fist. What could he say to her? That the idea now appealed to him? Alex coughed into his hand, attempting to force any words free. But they refused to part from his tongue, and he swallowed again.

"Forgive my outburst," she offered and placed a tentative hand on his arm. "I can tell by your unspoken words and features, the thought of taking a wife is terrifying. I must confess another flaw of mine is my quick temper and rash decisions. I fear 'tis one I'll always battle for control."

Flaw? Alex saw none in the beauty before him. Stubborn, brazen, willful. But flawed? Nae.

He gazed down at her small hand—the warmth seeping into his skin. Alex placed his hand over hers. "Much has occurred since that particular discussion with my brother."

Astonishment flared within her eyes. She squeezed his arm. "Them I am the fool for speaking harshly."

Chuckling softly, Alex released his hold on her hand and wrapped an arm around her waist. "I believe ye misunderstood what I shared with ye earlier."

Her gaze roamed over his features. When her lips parted, Alex battled for control. He would take no kisses until she came willingly to his bed.

"Then ye have not rejected the idea of marriage?"

"Nae," he confirmed, surprising himself with the declaration.

Aine grinned slowly, like the sun breaking through the clouds on a stormy day.

His heart fractured a little bit more. Raising his hand, Alex brushed his fingers over her soft cheeks. She turned and pressed a kiss along his palm. A groan of pleasure escaped from him, aching for her mouth to be somewhere else on his body.

When the flames snapped in the hearth, Aine's startled gasp severed the tender moment between them. "More mead?" she mumbled. Though she tried to compose herself, Alex noted her shaky movements.

"Allow me," he suggested.

After giving him a curt nod, Aine went to the chair by the fire.

"Who is Mab?" asked Alex, refilling their cups.

Tilting her head to the side, she replied, "An owl friend. Glenna brought her from the Fae realm when she arrived."

Crossing to her side, Alex handed her one of the cups. She acknowledged the gesture with a nod of thanks and another beaming smile.

Alex returned to the table. Grabbing another chair, he dragged it across the wooden floor. After settling down, he gazed at the lass over the rim of his cup. "So

Glenna is not half-human?"

Aine laughed, filling the room with her musical sound. "Goodness, nae."

After tucking a stray honeyed curl around her ear, she leaned forward as if she was going to impart a great secret. "Glenna is *hundreds* of years older than me. As a healer, the elders judged it wise to have a Fae from the realm to guide us with herbal knowledge. Her keen insight of the herbs used in Scotland is vast. We welcome her wisdom." She cast a furtive glance toward the door. "I consider Glenna like a sister. She assisted me through a dark time after my mother left."

Bracing his forearms onto his thighs, Alex stared into the glowing embers within the flames. He understood the loss of family profoundly. Each day, he struggled with Adam's departure into another time. Often, he'd wake in the middle of the night with an ache pressing against his chest. Never again would he ken what life Adam led in the future, or those of his brother's kin.

Aine set her cup on the floor. "Give me your hand."

He blinked several times. Without questioning her intent, he held his hand outward. He studied the lass while she cradled his hand and then traced two fingers in a circular pattern inside his palm. The warmth of mead, the fire, and her touch seeped into his skin. The tension across Alex's shoulders lessened.

Aine's eyes brimmed with tenderness when she spoke. "Ye are a warrior hardened by the death of one brother, *and* the loss of another. Unable to carve out your own plans, ye have remained silent while others ventured onward. Ye hide the pain deep—concealed from the world from all except me." She curved his fingers into his palm. "'Tis time ye reached for your destiny, Alex."

"What do ye ken of my pain, *leannán*?" he asked in a hushed voice.

A small smile of enchantment touched her lips. Reaching out, Aine tapped his upper arm. "Not only does your pain weave around your heart, but also as a warrior's band around here, showing me ye shall always grieve for another."

The cup slipped from his hand, dropping to the floor. "Grief is my shield. Not even Patrick witnessed my despair at times," he uttered in a voice haunted by the past.

A frown marred her features. Aine picked up his cup and leaned back in her chair. "Do ye fear more losses?"

He stood abruptly. "There will always be losses, battles, decisions made by others. As a chieftain, I cannot allow the fear to interfere with my duties. Ye have seen my anguish. Now I ask for ye to forget what ye have witnessed."

Rising slowly, Aine pressed her palm to his cheek. "Forgive me, once again. I overstepped by speaking to ye of what I sensed within your troubles." She laughed nervously. "This other gift can be *another flaw* of mine."

Alex merely studied her for a moment, thoughtfully, then turned and walked out of the house.

Chapter Eleven

"When the stars refuse to grant your wish, make another one." ~Fae Lore

Fighting the urge to smack Glenna with her pillow, Aine turned her back toward her friend. The woman's snores were loud enough to hail the Great Dragon who resided in the waters near Urquhart Castle in the Great Glen. Sleep might have lured her companion to a comfortable abyss, despite the small bed, but Aine found herself unable to succumb to any rest because of one man who stirred countless emotions inside her.

Alex.

She tucked a hand under the side of her face. Her gaze lingered along the massive shoulders of the man lying in front of the hearth. Though the flames had died down to embers, she noted the steady rise and fall of his chest. A smile curved the corners of her mouth as she swept her gaze to the sword positioned in front of him. Even in this shelter of peace, the warrior required his weapon in the event of an attack.

When he left the dwelling earlier, she yearned to run after him. But Glenna had made an appearance, and Aine resigned to leave him alone with his thoughts.

I should have remained silent and not offered my wisdom to ye, Alex.

Her heart constricted when she'd witnessed his pain.

Unable to offer any comfort, Aine sought to soothe his agony with her words.

Her uncle once confessed, *Everyone battles grief differently. Ye cannot mend all troubles, including Keegan's. Tend to your own.*

Aine let out a heavy sigh. *Ye were correct, Uncle.*

Glenna's snoring turned into a grumbled mix of words, and Aine whispered a curse.

Unable to find any rest, Aine slipped quietly from the furs. When her feet touched the chilled floor, she trembled and pressed a fist to her mouth. Reaching for another fur at the end of the bed, she padded silently toward the warmth of the dwindling fire.

Settling down on her side across from Alex, she wrapped the fur around her body and studied the man. Contentment filled his features—from his forehead to those full lips she ached to taste again. Her fingers twitched to brush aside a lock of dark hair that had fallen over his brow.

I wonder how many times your nose has been broken. In battles? In the lists? Fighting over a woman?

Aine didn't want to think of the women this man might have had. A pain of jealousy knifed through her. *For now, ye are my champion. My warrior. Many men sought to take me away, but none have entered into my heart like ye have.*

Powerless to stop the tide of feelings for Alex, she continued to explore the possibilities of a life with him outside Taloch. Would he be agreeable to stay with her? In a marriage?

"Return to the bed, Aine. Ye must try and get rest." His soft burr brushed over her like a warm caress.

Startled, Aine snorted, and then quickly placed a

hand over her mouth.

Alex cracked open one eye. "Ye find humor in my request?"

Shifting closer to him, Aine whispered, "Ye try sleeping next to someone whose snores can wake the bones from the dead."

Closing his eye, he shared, "Our youngest brother, Adam, was known to snore so loud ye could hear the sounds if ye were standing in the north tower. As a young lad, he'd sneak out at night and go to the river to skip stones over the water in the moonlight. The first time he slipped out of the castle, I followed the sound of his deep snores. Found him curled up asleep against a giant yew tree."

She chuckled low. "Was he good at skipping stones?"

Alex's face creased into a sudden smile. "Aye. The best of all of us."

To keep from reaching out to him, Aine dug her fingers into the fur. "I am glad your mind has healed. 'Tis good to remember fond memories."

He murmured an acknowledgement.

Resuming her gaze upon the man, Aine attempted to steady her breathing and racing heart. However, sleep did not beckon her. Instead, she flipped onto her back and gazed up at the ceiling, attempting to count the many knots in the wood. An owl hooted in the far distance, and she pondered if Mab had returned from her quest to Taloch. Would the day dawn with sun or more snow?

Embers snapped inside the hearth, and she shivered. The cold seeped into her feet. Trying to adjust the fur over her toes did not ease the chill.

"Aine?" he whispered softly.

She turned her head toward him. "Aye?"

"Let me offer ye the warmth of my body," he suggested, his gaze dark and compelling.

Licking her lips, she muttered, "I thank ye, but nae."

"Either ye come closer, or I shall relinquish my covering to ye." He pushed aside his sword and patted the floor between them.

Indecision plagued her. She stewed for a moment and considered returning to the bed. But Glenna's snores became even more persistent. And if she declined Alex's generous offer of a covering, then the man would get no more rest.

Blowing out an irritated breath, Aine finally relented. She scooted near the man and turned her back to him. When his arm wrapped around her waist in a leisurely hold, she stiffened. What would Glenna think if she woke? To find Aine in the arms of a man?

The rumble of his laughter rippled against her back. Aine fisted her hands.

Alex leaned near her ear. "Did ye think I would ravish ye here? With our present company?"

Embarrassed, she shook her head in response.

"Trust me, if we were alone, I would be sorely tempted to take ye." He breathed the words across her neck, sending warmth down her spine. "Relax, and sleep will come," he urged.

Alex's heat and scent surrounded her—filling her with a need for the promises yet to be fulfilled. Nevertheless, her warrior proved correct. Relaxing her fingers, she steadied her breathing. Blissful heat swept throughout her limbs with each breath.

On a sigh, Aine's eyes fluttered closed, and she surrendered to the embrace of deep slumber.

****

Shrill birdsong echoed within Aine's dreams. She fought to return to the warrior who held her within his strong arms. To stroke her hand over his broad chest and along his massive shoulders. Yet the bird's chatter shattered the blissful moment—the sound hammering with determination within her ears.

"Go away," she mumbled. Her hand reached out, seeking the warmth of the man. When she encountered the rough, cold floor, she blinked in confusion. Bolting upright, she brushed the hair that had escaped from her braids away from her face. Her sight rested on the man standing in front of the window.

Stifling a yawn, Aine stretched out her legs and stood. She grabbed the fur, wrapping the covering around her chilled body. With quiet steps, she made her way toward Alex.

"'Tis a good morn?" she whispered, glancing outward through the partially open shutters. The twinkling star remained the last guard from the night sky while she watched its light slowly vanish with the dawn.

"We can return to Taloch," Alex uttered softly.

When she looked up at him, Aine noted the dark smudges under his eyes. "Did ye not sleep well?"

He arched a brow while a smiled curved his mouth. "With ye in my arms? Nae."

Heat crept up the back of her neck with the understanding of his meaning. She nudged him slightly with her elbow. "I should not have accepted your offer for warmth."

Alex pointed over his shoulder. "And stay with your companion who snores as loud as my horse? Thank the Gods she finally quieted."

Aine cupped a hand over mouth to suppress the giggles. "Truth? Beast snores?"

Clasping his hands behind his back, he nodded. "Something fierce."

"At least tonight ye can find rest in your own bed," she said, though an ache to be parted from him, even at night, unsettled Aine.

He reached out and tugged on a loose curl. "Are ye certain I'll find rest? Perchance I will dream of holding ye in my arms again."

Biting her lower lip, Aine returned her attention out the window. *I have done nothing but dream of ye every night, Alex.* Flustered, she complained, "I present a wretched mess this morning."

Alex leaned near her ear. "Ye are a beauty, Aine. One day, I am going to tell ye what to do with these honeyed curls."

She dared not look at the man. If she did, Aine would demand Alex tell her exactly what he meant. And then she'd want him to show her. Now.

"I'll go check on the horses," he announced, stepping away from her.

After the door closed behind him, Aine let out the breath she'd been holding and lowered her head. *What am I going to do with ye, Alex? Will I truly allow ye to come to my bed, and then risk having my heart cleaved in two?*

She laughed quietly to cover her annoyance. *Ye ask questions ye already ken the answers.*

"Did ye find comfort and rest in the man's arms, Aine?"

Startled, she snapped her head up. "Are ye scolding me? Alex remained honorable." Aine dared not mention how she felt the man's hard length along her back before she'd drifted off to sleep.

Glenna smirked and stretched her arms overhead. "I come from a realm where many Fae seek their passions in the Pleasure Gardens, including me. Nae, Aine. Merely surprised ye took so long to sneak from my bed."

Turning toward the woman, she hesitated, measuring her for a moment. "What happens in the Pleasure Gardens?"

A smile quirked around the corners of Glenna's mouth. "Wonderous delights. But this is not the Fae realm, Aine."

Nodding in understanding, she retreated to the hearth and dumped wood onto the cold ashes.

Glenna approached by her side. Blowing across her palm, the wood burst into flames.

Glancing sharply at the woman, Aine tried to fathom why she'd used her magic.

"To answer your unspoken question, I am permitted to use my power. Occasionally. And 'tis bloody cold in here." Her friend put an arm around Aine's shoulders. "Do ye care for the man?"

Aine laughed nervously.

Glenna released her hold. "Should I worry he has already taken your maidenhead, and ye found nae passion? Or the man does not care for ye? Though by the continued looks he gives only ye, I might be wrong."

"Nae, he has not bedded me," blurted out Aine. She crossed to one of the chairs and sat, tucking her feet under her.

"But do ye care for him?" prodded Glenna softly.

Aine sighed. "Care for the man? From the moment he stepped between the giant oaks." She pounded her fist against her chest. "My heart beats fierce each time Alex enters a room. I am quick to anger, spout my opinion, and find I'm unable to control the countless feelings coursing through me." She swallowed, then lowered her voice. "My body aches in places I long to have him touch."

Kneeling in front of her, Glenna took her hands. "Aye, ye have this burning to be with Alex."

"'Tis far worse," lamented Aine, watching as the flames grew larger within the hearth.

"Worse?" echoed the woman, dropping her hands and rising. "What could possibly be worse than—"

"I believe I love him," interrupted Aine, staring at her friend. Unable to stop the flow of words, her confession startled herself.

Glenna's eyes widened in alarm, followed by a burst of rich laughter. "Oh, Aine Fraser! How can *love* be worse?"

"But I have only known Alex for a brief time," argued Aine. "Should we not spend additional time together? I am uncertain of these new feelings."

Glenna's eyes brimmed with tenderness. "We never are prepared when love strikes us with its arrow into our heart. For some, love blossoms over time, others the emotion bursts forth the instant two people meet. Sadly, there are a few who never get to experience the first blush or long-lasting effects of love's power."

Before Aine had a chance to utter another word of protest, the woman dashed over to a set of shelves by her worktable. She stood on her tiptoes in search of something. "I ken 'tis here," she mused, pushing aside jars of herbs and salves. "Unless Keegan dared to venture inside my home and take the bottle."

Curious, Aine rose from her chair. After folding the fur and placing the covering on the chair, she ambled to the woman's side. "What are ye looking for?"

"This," she announced in triumph. "A special crafted mead from the home of the Dragon Knights. Alastair MacKay blends one of the best meads in all of Scotland. Even better than in my world."

Aine shrugged. "I do not understand why this is important."

Her friend pinched her arm. "'Tis cause to celebrate!"

"Goodness!" She blew out a frustrated breath and started to unravel her tangled braids. "I think I shall go slice the loaf of bread I brought. Clearly, ye deem it necessary to drink in celebration to what I have shared with ye."

Glenna clucked her tongue in disapproval. "When *love* enters your heart, ye cannot blow the feeling to the winds like the seeds of a dandelion."

Aine's hands stilled. "I never spouted—"

"Love is a reason to *celebrate*," she interjected. "The emotion can cast ye to the stars or send ye hurtling across a stormy sea sinking ye into its depths." In a more somber tone, Glenna added, "Love is the greatest power to possess. Once ye have tasted the feeling, ye can never return to your former self. Many men have passed through Taloch, and none have stirred ye *or* caused ye to become unsettled."

Watching as the woman poured the special mead into two cups, Aine asked, "But what if he does not love me?"

Glenna gave her a skeptical glance. "If I ken anything about men, Aine, I am certain there is more to

Alex MacFhearguis than his desire to simply bed ye. Not only does he look like he wants to devour ye, but also to protect ye." Handing a cup to Aine, she smiled knowingly. "I do not reckon he understands his own emotions either."

Taking the offered drink, Aine mused, "Then what should I do? What if Rory returns and sends Alex back through the veil without me? What if the other elders are furious over what I have done and decide to keep me from entering his Scotland?"

Glenna regarded her thoughtfully. "Do not worry. I assume Rory will be in long talks with the elders. At least until midwinter. This will provide ye and Alex additional time to spend with each other."

Smiling, Aine said, "Thank ye for speaking with me."

"One more piece of wisdom, Aine. A Fae's love is eternal. And ye are half-Fae. I deem ye have found true love. Now ye must determine if love shall be returned to ye." The woman raised her cup. "Until then, we have a feast to prepare for."

Chapter Twelve

"When ye find your path shrouded in mists, send forth the falcon of wisdom to clear your vision."
~MacFhearguis Motto

Alex knuckled his eyes and ran a hand through his hair, ridding the last traces of what little sleep he found from his weary mind. Heaving a sigh, he braced his forearms on the wooden ledge.

The morning dawned cold throughout Taloch, especially inside the gatehouse. He'd always prefer this time alone—to greet the new day in silence. Marveling at the peaceful scene around him, he cast his gaze outward. When the sun rose, the light spilled across the treetops. Since Taloch was nestled below the mountainside between peaks overlooking the ancient trees, the gatehouse proved to be an excellent vantage to witness the dawn.

Upon their return from the healer's home, Aine called a meeting with her uncle, Keegan, and the other few men. With her urging, Alex presented his ideas about making Taloch a protective and learning castle— one that would be suitable even in his Scotland. After all agreed to his plans, work began on the building of a portcullis. His many days had been spent assisting Keegan and the other men, but Alex's nights brought no comfort or rest. Aine slipped into his thoughts and haunted his dreams. He'd wake in a burning condition, refusing to find release in stroking his cock.

"Aine, *leannán*. How much longer can I control my desire for ye? Ye stir my blood to a fever."

And there remained the thorn for countless sleepless nights. A lass who shattered all his protective shields with one look while in a corridor, a gentle touch over his hand in passing within the bailey, or a seductive smile when she brought him a jug of mead.

She left him without words and breath. A wee lass who also banished the ache of loneliness and soothed the anguished beast within his soul.

He smacked the wood with his fist. "Ye are nae a young lad hungry to taste your first woman," chastised Alex into the frosty air. But Aine proved to be no ordinary lass.

Even in the quiet stillness of his surroundings, Alex tried to quell another uneasiness inside him. Rory MacGregor continued to be absent. Neither the man nor any messages were received. No one appeared concerned, not even Aine. With midwinter two days away, surely the Fae warrior would make an appearance. Though she told him time moved differently, Alex constantly worried about his brother and those within Leòmhann.

He laughed bitterly. "Ye may not have wanted to rule Leòmhann, *Brother*, but I pray ye are faring well."

Alex stiffened, instinctively placing his fingers over the hilt of his sword. His keen senses alerted him to the intruder ascending into the gatehouse. He inhaled sharply and smiled. Relaxing his grip on the blade, he welcomed the beauty entering the small enclosure.

Aine's smile warmed the chill from his body. "A

good morn to ye. I ken ye have not broken your fast, so I thought to bring ye some porridge and a jug of cider. If ye prefer ale, I shall fetch a fresh jug."

Surprised by the gesture, Alex motioned toward the bench sitting against the back of the wall. "Nae. This will be sufficient. Ye are most kind."

After hastily placing the small bowl and jug onto the bench, Aine removed a cup from the belt at her waist and filled it with cider. "I welcome your opinion on your meal." She pressed the cup into his hands.

"Is there a reason why? Have ye put maggots in my porridge?" He took a sip of the cool liquid and then placed the cup down.

Her expression darkened. "Never would I think to foul a meal. I have enough problems tending to *any* food in the kitchens."

Choking back the laughter, Alex turned away from her. As he reached for the bowl of porridge, the mixed aroma of apples, honey, and hazelnuts filled him. His stomach growled in anticipation. Picking up the large spoon on the side, he took a mouthful, savoring the flavors. "Mmm…"

"From the sound ye are making, I assume ye like the porridge? Or is this not to your liking? Some men prefer to break their fast with meat and cheese."

When he turned around, Alex held out a spoonful to Aine. "I must compliment the person responsible for making a delicious meal. And I have nae preference for certain food requests."

Her features beamed, and Alex smiled in return. "Are ye the person?" he asked.

She nodded, shoving back the hood of her cloak. He sucked in a breath. Her hair spilled over her shoulders and down to her breasts in a waterfall of honeyed curls. The dawn's early light shimmered off her locks, holding Alex captive.

Opening her mouth, she allowed Alex to guide the spoon he held past her lips.

Aine smacked her lips in obvious pleasure. "With the help of Rowena, I made ye a simple fare. First time I did not scorch the food," she acknowledged with a look of pride.

"'Tis good," he commented in a hoarse voice, content to watch her savor the meal. In truth, he'd eat anything the lass presented to him, even a hardened and burned bannock.

Alex scooped another portion and held out the offering to her.

"Nae," she argued. "After ye have taken more."

Quickly complying, he devoured the spoonful. "Now ye," he urged, presenting another offering of more porridge.

She laughed. "One more, but the remainder is yours." After Aine ate the bit of porridge from the spoon, a morsel dripped onto her chin.

And Alex wasted no time. Dropping the spoon back into his meal, he swiftly cupped her soft chin. Her eyes widened in surprise. Lowering his head, he licked the morsel free from her skin. "Ye missed some."

"Alex." She breathed his name on a sigh. "Are ye certain I did not miss another crumb?"

"Aye," he confirmed, turning her head slightly. He nuzzled her neck. Slowly, Alex pressed a kiss against the pulsing vein along her warm skin.

"More," she begged.

Grinning, Alex asked, "Food *or* kisses?"

She trembled beneath his touch. Swiftly removing the bowl from his hand, Aine tossed the meal out the gatehouse opening. "Does that answer your question?"

Alex drew back and arched a brow. "Ye should not waste food."

Placing her hands against his chest, she shrugged. "One of the animals will finish what little is remaining. And if ye want more, I will gladly fetch another bowl."

He wrapped an arm around her waist. With his other hand, he stroked the pad of his thumb over her full bottom lip. Desire slammed into him.

"Kiss me, Alex," she whispered.

He shook his head slowly. Instead, he placed feather-like kisses on her eyelids, nose, and along the softness below her ears. Aine moaned in pleasure while he continued to explore other areas to kiss the lass.

Grabbing her hand, Alex traced his tongue along the inside of her wrist, ending with a searing kiss.

"Ye are tormenting me," protested Aine, her breathing labored. "I can...cannot understand what is happening to me. My body burns in places I do not fathom."

He lifted his hooded gaze. "Did ye forget my vow?"

Standing on her tiptoes, she nipped with her teeth along his bearded chin. "One kiss is all I ask."

Alex let out a growl. Tugging on her hand, he led her to the wooden bench. After he sat down, he brought her across his lap. "Never have I broken a vow, *leannán*. Until now."

"And I shall not release ye. Your vow to me will be my gift to ye." Aine wrapped her arms around his neck.

A thorny mix of feelings settled in his gut like gnarled vines. "What are ye saying, Aine?"

Her silky voice held a challenge. "I want to come to your chamber tonight. I desire ye to give me pleasure—to show me how to please a man—to please *ye*." Aine tugged on the strings of his tunic while keeping her focus on him. "I ken ye have bedded other women, but do ye think ye could forget about them when we are together?"

Alex's hand shook as he grabbed a fistful of her curls. "When I take ye, Aine, there shall be nae others. Ever." Surprisingly, the declaration did not bother him.

Her smile broadened in approval. "Then I shall expect ye after the evening meal. We are savoring a light fare in preparation for the feast. Now kiss me, my warrior."

Alex's heart pounded fiercely against his chest. Never had he lost control with any woman. Never. Duty demanded from him as a young lad led him to a trained warrior in tactics—hardened by conflicts and skilled in command. Yet now, Alex no longer battled against leaving or the consequences. He gave no care if the world shattered around them. All he desired was the woman with beguiling eyes sitting in his lap. And the crack in his armor split more.

She had presented herself as a gift—one he fully intended on savoring tonight. A gift Alex did not deserve. But by the Gods, he'd feast on her body until he'd fulfilled her request.

Without another thought, Alex moved his mouth over hers, devouring the softness of her lips. She opened fully, darting her tongue against his. The kiss spiraled through his blood, tempting him beyond reason. The touch of her lips on his sent a shock wave through his body. Releasing his hold on her hair, he then cupped the back of her head and deepened the kiss, savoring apples, honey, and her own sweet scent.

When Aine shifted on his lap, moving in a slow rhythm, Alex growled low.

His cock strained to be freed—to sink into her soft womanly folds. "My body burns for only ye," he murmured, breaking free from her luscious lips.

Aine whimpered, burying her head into his neck. "I ache, as well," she whispered.

"Show me where?" he urged, stroking a finger down the curve of her cheek.

When she lifted her head, her eyes gleamed with a lust that mirrored his own. "Between my legs." A rosy stain blossomed from her neck to cover her entire face.

His look became predatory. Determined to ease the agony and give her a sample of what to expect tonight, Alex moved his hand beneath her gown to skim his fingers over her thigh. "Do ye trust me, *leannán*?"

She shivered but made no move to shrug out of his grasp. "Always," she responded.

Her freely given trust in Alex undid him. Holding her in his arms, he knew then he could never willingly be parted from her. He'd protect Aine until his dying breath. He'd cherish her with each kiss, each stroke of his hand.

"Keep your eyes on mine," he ordered in a low voice.

Aine bit her lower lip.

As his fingers skimmed a path up her thigh, he watched while her breathing hitched, and her eyes widened. Her heat surrounded his hand. Slowly, Alex brushed his fingers over her damp curls and parted her sweet folds.

She squirmed under his touch. "What are ye doing?"

"Is this where ye ache, *leannán*?" he asked, while his caress explored the center between her creamy thighs.

She inhaled sharply. "Aye, *aye*." Her hands lowered to his shoulders.

"'Tis your sweet bud that I shall pleasure," he rasped out. His finger lightly rubbed the hard nub, and Aine moaned.

Alex continued with his pleasurable assault, stroking and teasing her core, until she leaned forward and kissed the side of his neck. His hand stilled while he let out a guttural groan.

"More," she pleaded in desperation. "I need more of ye."

Reaching for a fistful of her curls, Alex yanked her head away from his neck. "Ye are a siren—*my* siren."

"Always yours," she avowed, never straying from his gaze. Her eyes glistened like starlight. Aine sealed her vow with a passionate kiss that pierced straight to his heart.

When his finger delved inside her, her grip on his shoulders tightened. A gasp of pleasure fell from her lips, and her nails dug deeper into his cloak.

"Ye are so soft, my *leannán*. I long to taste your sweetness. Will ye yield to me?"

"*Anything*, Alex. Just end this torment," she sobbed out.

"Keep your focus on me," he demanded in a rough voice.

While the tide of her passion built, his grew stronger. Beads of sweat broke out across Alex's forehead. The blood hammered inside his veins. His body shook with an ancient need to possess Aine, and his cock swelled to an unbearable ache to sink into her heated core.

"Oh, *Alex*," she cried out, riding the tide of passion.

He captured her scream with his mouth, stealing her breath and returning it mingled with his own. Her cries of passion echoed deep within his body and filled his head with her musical sound. Her breathing was ragged as Alex gently removed his fingers from her heated core and straightened her gown and cloak.

Finally spent, Aine collapsed against his chest.

Alex tried to quiet his trembling body and hers while wrapping a protective arm around her body. His gaze drifted outward toward the trees. Though he had not found his own release, a small sense of peace settled inside him. There would be ample time tonight to enjoy his own passion.

A bird fluttered between the branches of a tree, finally landing on one of the limbs—heralding the new day with a song.

Leaning his head back against the wood, he marveled at the beauty of his surroundings, including the woman in his arms. Unlike most of the women he bedded, Aine stormed into his life and heart. Often, Alex preferred his women quiet, submissive, and agreeable to his desires. One night of slaking his needs was sufficient. He didn't possess elegant words like his brother Patrick to lure women. And he certainly did not ken the secret for keeping a woman in his company for any length of time.

Nevertheless, the Fae beauty snuggled against him altered the man he used to be. She slashed away the darkness with one radiant smile. Aine saw beyond the beast lurking in the shadows and found the man.

When the time comes to depart Taloch, soon, ye will come with me, Aine.

Raising her head, she murmured, "What are ye thinking?"

He chuckled low. "Nothing important."

"Did ye ken your eyes glow more amber when ye tell a lie?"

"Are ye using your Fae gifts?" he chided.

Her smiled faded. Brushing a lock of hair away from his eye, she said, "I would never attempt to look inside someone's mind."

Alex's brow furrowed.

"To clarify," began Aine, then cleared her throat. "If I had the ability to see inside your mind, I would not do so."

Kissing her lips softly, he breathed the answer to her earlier question across her mouth. "How to leave this haven and take ye with me."

Chapter Thirteen

"Be wary when a white stag wanders between the ancient forest. If he dips his antlers, the path is not for ye." ~Fae Lore

Shoving aside the cup of mead, Alex stared across the length of the great hall in an effort to ignore the man sitting to his left. Large trenchers filled with fish, fowl, and meat were carefully placed along the tables by younger women and children. Soon, larger trenchers with cabbages, onions, wild mushrooms, and other root vegetables were settled beside all the meats. A few of the men brought in jugs of fresh mead and ale—smiling and bantering with each other. The mood appeared lighthearted for a meal prior to midwinter.

Yet ye have nae worries here with an abundant food pantry. Taloch has not suffered the harshness of cruel battles or the loss of crops during a fierce storm.

Alex tried not to groan when Eamon continued his persistent discussion of disbanding the need to fortify the south side of Taloch. He argued the addition of the portcullis would deter any enemy. Therefore, they should not spend additional time and materials strengthening a fortress which would never witness a battle.

Alex firmly disagreed. After giving Eamon his reasonings once more, the man continued to plague him with further arguments. A dull ache settled behind Alex's eyes.

Keegan wove his way between the people carrying two jugs within his arms. Setting them down on the table in front of Alex, he pointed to his cup. "Do ye not care for the mead?"

Alex folded his arms over his chest. "'Tis good."

The man peered inside Alex's cup. "Have ye drank any?"

"'Tis my second cup," he lied, not wanting to dull his senses. His thoughts were on another tasty meal later with a certain lass. And he'd planned to enjoy her fully without the dulling effects of any mead or ale.

"Nae," challenged Eamon, nudging him with his elbow. "Ye have taken only a sip."

Again, Alex, argued, "Ye did not see me down a cup earlier."

Eamon shifted in his chair, staring at Alex like he'd sprouted horns. "Did we not come in together?"

The dull ache was now replaced with a throbbing pain inside his head. "Aye, but ye were speaking with Hamish."

"While I poured ye a cup of mead," retorted Eamon.

"Your attention happened to be fixed on the lad while ye were correcting him on the ways to enter the hall," corrected Alex. A muscle twitched in his jaw as he fought to remain seated and endure this foolish bantering over the amount of mead he'd consumed.

Keegan snorted. Reaching for a jug, he filled one of the empty cups to the brim. Raising it high, he looked directly at Alex. "Let us drink to welcome the coming of midwinter."

By the Gods, where are ye, Aine? Save me from this

torture.

Eamon's mouth took an unpleasant twist. "I am not addled to forget this is your first cup, MacFhearguis."

"Why, Uncle, ye appear to be displeased with our guest. Allow me to refill your cup, and we shall all drink as one."

Alex held back the curse he wanted to fling out. His jaw clenched so tightly he feared it would shatter. *This is madness. If ye do not arrive soon, Aine, I am coming to fetch ye.*

Apparently, Keegan had already been sampling several cups of mead by the way he filled his uncle's cup. The liquid sloshed over the rim and onto the table.

Eamon directed his ire toward his nephew. "Might I ask how many cups ye have drank?"

Keegan gave the man a wink. "Ye ken everyone is already celebrating." He lifted his cup outward. "Do ye not do so in your Scotland, Alex?"

His uncle looked affronted. "We are in Taloch."

Tempering his fury, Alex decided to join forces with Keegan. Reaching for his cup, he declared, "To the midwinter. Warmth, food, drink, *and* the blessings of the Gods and Goddesses."

Eamon's features softened. "Indeed. To Mother Danu."

"May she continue to protect us," added Keegan before draining his cup.

"Aye," acknowledged Alex.

Laughter carried over the din of the others inside the hall. Before Alex had a chance to partake of his mead, he sought out the woman with the musical voice and found her weaving along the long tables, carrying a basket of breads. Aine's soft curls flowed gently down to her waist with each sway of her hips.

Alex took a swallow of mead and promptly set the cup down. Rising abruptly, he waited patiently for her to approach. Grateful for the empty chair on his right, he placed a protective hand on the smooth wooden back, making certain no one but Aine would sit beside him.

When Keegan's good humor vanished, Alex gave no regard as to what he thought of him. The man already appeared addled from too much drink and proved no threat. Alex grew weary of hiding what he felt inside his heart. Though he'd steeled the emotion away from the others, he sought to share the revelation with only one. The beauty striding toward him.

A young girl halted Aine's progress to him, asking her a question about the honey. Aine's eyes alighted with mirth. Alex's fingers dug into the wood, waiting. When Aine cupped a hand over her mouth in amusement, he didn't fight the smile forming on his mouth. After giving the girl a kiss on the cheek, Aine finally made her way to him. The breath he'd been holding back eased forth.

Alex took the basket of bread from her arms. "I have saved ye a seat next to me," he murmured softly. He quickly placed the basket on the table and pulled out the chair.

Her eyes held his for a moment. "Ye are kind," she stated, settling in beside him.

Reaching for a jug, Alex filled a cup for her. "Your brother assures me this mead is the best."

"Keegan believes *all* the mead made here is the best, regardless of the maker," she grumbled feebly, taking a sip from her cup.

"Has he sampled the one from Alastair MacKay?"

Aine plucked a hazelnut from a nearby trencher.

"Nae. Glenna refuses to share anything from outside Taloch."

Shifting in his chair, he asked, "Then why did she share her mead from the MacKay with us?"

She swept him a captivating smile. "I believe Glenna likes ye."

"The woman approves of me? With ye?" Resisting the urge to grab her hand, Alex kept his hands fisted within his lap.

Amusement flickered in Aine's eyes. "Ye appear surprised."

Alex let out a garbled response. "*Aye*." He hesitated before reaching for his cup. Taking a small sip, he added, "Did she mention anything else about me?"

"Are ye more concerned with her opinion than mine?" Humor laced her question while she popped the nut into her mouth.

He choked on the mead. "The lion of Leòmhann has never been favored among the Fae. Even though my brother is a Dragon Knight."

Aine gasped, reaching out to touch his hand. "Sweet Goddess! Now I ken your sorrow. Your brother is a Dragon Knight, though lives in another time. He started the new order of Knights."

Smiling weakly, he confirmed, "Aye, Adam."

"The Fae speak praises of *all* the Dragon Knights," she declared, removing her hand from his.

"But I am not a Dragon Knight."

"Nevertheless, ye are his kin and should be respected," she returned.

He bent his head near hers. "For tonight, let us not speak of sorrows *or* Dragon Knights."

Aine grinned over the rim of her cup. "Agreed. Only

pleasures."

****

Pacing in front of the hearth, Alex tried to settle his impatience. The moon had entered the night sky hours ago, and Aine had not arrived in his chamber. A jug of mead and ale set on a table, tempting him to quench the dryness inside his parched mouth and soothe the anxiety coursing through his veins.

Rubbing a hand over his brow, he sought to focus on the flames snapping within the hearth. Yet they merely added to his angst. In frustration, Alex yanked the tunic over his head and tossed the garment onto the floor. Storming to the window, he drew back one of the shutters and inhaled sharply. An icy blast of air slapped at his face, cooling the raging beast within him.

Within moments, his uneasiness quieted. His gaze drifted upward to the numerous stars draped against an inky black sky. How different they were than in his home. Vast and appearing to be arranged in a distinctive pattern. The more he studied them, the more his heart settled.

Alex peered over his shoulder at the wooden door. "Were ye prevented from venturing away, my *leannán*?"

All throughout the meal, Aine explained to him of the many celebrations leading up to midwinter. Days were spent honoring the Oak and Holly Kings, along with the light that would soon usher in a new season. Tomorrow, the hall would be graced with pine branches, ribbons, apples, and other festive garlands.

Alex boasted of Leòmhann's festivities, especially with the arrival of Patrick's wife, Gwen. But within the gates of Taloch, these people regarded the midwinter with great merry-making. All work ceased, and everyone—from the youngest to the oldest—brought a joyfulness to the season.

Returning his sight to the moonlight within the sky, he heaved a heavy sigh. "Did ye change your mind, Aine?"

He smiled when he heard the door open and close behind him.

"Ye would doubt my feelings for ye, my warrior?" questioned the familiar soft voice.

Alex turned around. He gaped at the beauty inside his chamber, leaning against the closed door. He swallowed. "Nae, but I grew impatient."

Slowly, she pushed back the hood of her cloak. "As did I. However, I had to attend to most of the children before I sought out my chamber in preparation."

"Preparation," he echoed, while another blast of freezing air smacked along his back.

Her hands twisted in front of her. "I cannot stop this quaking in my body. I tried to ease the trembling with soothing herbs, but I can think of nothing else but being in your arms again. And now with ye standing there without your tunic…" She paused and took a hesitant step forward. "I find my *breathing* is labored, and my heart unsteady."

A tremor of longing rippled through him. With relaxed strides, Alex closed the distance between them. He took her small hands into his powerful grip. Brushing his thumbs over her soft skin, he lowered his head near her ear. "Are ye truly ready for the pleasures I shall give ye, *leannán*? If ye are uncertain, now is the time to speak."

She lifted her head and met his heated gaze. "Did I not give ye my vow—my *gift* to ye?"

Alex dropped her hands. "Once I bolt the door, there is nae leaving. Do ye ken my meaning?"

Aine unclasped her cloak. The garment slid off her shoulders and fell to the floor.

With nothing but a thin chemise spilling down to above her delicate feet, Alex's gaze roamed lazily over her creamy neck to her pert nipples teasing him through the garment. In one swift move, he reached around her and bolted the door.

Aine twined her arms about his neck. "I am yours." The look he gave her pierced her soul—raw and compelling.

"How I have longed to see your hair spilling over your bare skin." His breath was hot between the curve of her neck and shoulder.

Alex's mouth took hers with a hunger both fierce and tender, in a kiss that sent her senses spiraling. His hands burned through the fabric of her chemise, and she desired her warrior more than the air she breathed. He smothered her mouth with demanding skill, thrusting his tongue deep inside. Aine surrendered to him, and the tide of passion swept her up in its current.

He slowly backed her across the chamber until they came to his bed. Without breaking the kiss, he brought her back onto the furs. His kisses were divine ecstasy, heating her body to an exquisite fervor which could not be quenched. Placing kisses at the hollow of her throat, he continued to make his way down until he came to her aching breasts, eager for his touch. She watched in a haze while his teeth grazed over the material and then freed first one breast and then the other.

Squirming beneath him, she moaned, attempting to free her arms.

He lifted his head. "Beauty." His hooded gaze was predatory, seductive, and she welcomed being captive to whatever passions he awoke within her.

While he renewed his pleasurable assault on her breasts, Aine found her body fevered, and a throbbing pulsed within her intimate area. "Rid me of this garment," she begged, yearning to feel his skin against hers.

On a growl, Alex ripped the chemise down the middle, freeing her from the agony of being trapped.

She gasped, but a sensuous smile curved her lips.

With deft skill, he undid the laces of his trews and eased them down his long legs. He swiftly stepped out and kicked them aside.

Her mouth became dry, gazing upon his hardened length.

Alex stroked himself, and her body clenched with need. "Does this please ye? Do ye wish for more?" The timbre of his voice flowed over her skin. The man appeared carved by the Gods as he stood before her with his lustful stance and hooded gaze.

Desire kept her tongue silent, and she simply nodded her approval for him to continue. His amber eyes darkened more with desire as he stalked toward her. Like the lion he spoke about, Alex loomed over her, trapping her beneath him. While his hand caressed her thigh, he nuzzled kisses along her neck. Her body trembled—going from half-ice to half-flame. His intimate touch left her breathing heavily, and when his finger swept across her sensitive core, Aine arched in pure pleasure. He took his time pressing kisses over her breasts and across the curve of her hip.

"I yearn to taste the sweetness between your soft

curls." When he nudged her thighs apart with his hands, his tongue traced a path over her stomach and farther down. After placing a gentle kiss on each of her thighs, he then blew against her intimate core. Her breathing came out in short gasps, trying to grasp the elusive flame. Yet when his tongue flicked over her center, Aine thought she'd died.

"*Alex*?" Her question half-sob, half-moan.

Words failed Aine as the man kept stroking the spark of passion within her. Desperation clawed at her in a wild tempest. Alex showered her with more kisses, licks, and nips with his teeth over her delicate area. The fever built and spread throughout her. A pulse of need drummed between her legs, and she groaned deeply. The tight knot within her begged for release, and she whimpered. When his moan rumbled deep against her, Aine closed her eyes and soared on the pleasurable tide, crying out his name as the tremors shook her body.

"*My Aine*," he whispered against her ear.

Alex's mouth captured her lips in a firestorm of passion. When he nudged her thighs farther apart with his knee, she felt the heat of his arousal near her entrance.

"Cannot hold back," he growled against her neck.

Wrapping her arms around his neck, she urged, "Take me now." She demanded with a fierceness that stunned her.

Taking her mouth in a savage kiss, Alex entered her in one swift thrust.

Aine hissed as pain and pleasure battled for control within her.

He froze his movements and began to ease back. Indecision wavered within his eyes.

"Do not stop," she ordered, digging her nails into his

shoulders.

Alex let out a groan and complied.

When he slid back inside, Aine began to find her own rhythm. He stroked the passion of desire once again with each thrust, kiss, and touch of his hands. She fisted her hands into his long hair, urging him onward. Dizziness swamped her vision as a wave of immeasurable pleasure tore through her body. He captured her scream with his mouth as she spiraled into an abyss of passion she'd never experienced.

Alex broke the connection with her lips. His guttural cry of release surrounded her, filling her completely. He shook while burying his head against her shoulder.

With slow movements, he rolled over onto his back, bringing her along with him. Alex cradled her against his chest—tugging on her curls with his free hand. She was blissfully content within his massive arms. Soon, her breathing found its natural rhythm, and Aine let out a sigh.

"Wonderous," she murmured, snuggling more against her warrior. She traced a finger along the scarred flesh that marred several areas on his chest. *What skirmishes have ye fought, my warrior?*

The rumble of his low laughter flowed over her. Raising her head, Aine furrowed her brow. "Were ye not pleased? I ken this is not your first time—"

Alex placed a finger over her lips. "*Pleased*? Ye are like a breath of spring air after a warm rain and as heady as the first scent of a rose. Ye have given this thorny and dark man a gift I do not deserve, *leannán*."

Her eyes misted with unshed tears. The shock of his declaration caused words Aine wanted to profess to remain wedged within her throat. Instead, she pressed her cheek against Alex's chest, listening to his heartbeat.

I love ye, my warrior—my champion. I have spread my wishes along your path. Do not crush them in anger as ye seek the journey in your heart.

Chapter Fourteen

"Your heart does not belong to ye but to your clan."
~MacFhearguis Motto

The sun rose in a splendid arc of light on the midwinter morning—glittering across the bridge leading into Taloch. Alex lifted his face to the warmth and inhaled deeply. Silently, he sent his prayers outward to the Gods and Goddesses, thanking them for a renewed sense of peace within him, and for the woman who'd entered his heart.

Since their night together, Alex hadn't a chance to speak alone with Aine. The preparations for the feast had begun in earnest throughout the castle the following morning. Yesterday was fraught with the continued building of the portcullis. He'd spent most of the day with Gordon in the forge. When Keegan wandered inside late in the morning with additional questions on the proportions, Alex almost let out a groan of displeasure.

Alex had hoped Aine would have changed her mind to assist in the forge. Yet his *leannán* had promptly informed all within hearing she would not be assisting in the gate building. Her tasks were required in the kitchens and adorning the great hall with more pine boughs.

Even when he went to her chamber late last night, he found her asleep curled up on a chair near the hearth. Scooping her into his arms, Alex tucked her beneath the furs in her bed and quietly left, returning to his own chamber.

Sleep did not beckon him. Her scent lingered everywhere in his bed. And dreams of their time together haunted him. *There is much I wish to share in my heart with ye, Aine. But I'm unable to find the words.*

"'Tis a good man who greets the midwinter with the first blush of dawn," announced Eamon, striding forth from the trees bordering the castle.

"Ye have risen early," remarked Alex with a smile.

"I have chosen to cleanse my body in the stream along with offering my prayers to the Goddess."

"In the icy water?" Alex barked out in laughter. "Did ye manage to dip your toe in the water and call it bathing?"

Eamon scratched the side of his face. "Forsooth, I built a fire to take the bitter chill from my bones afterward." He tilted his head to the side. "Ye should consider ridding the grime from yourself."

Alex winced. The thought of washing in a frigid stream held no appeal. To banish the sleep from his face, aye, but nothing else. He fisted his hands on his hips. "Nae. Perchance a tub filled with hot water, but I'll wait until winter thaws and the stream warms."

The man raked a hand through his damp hair. "Did ye ken there is a giant wooden tub across from my solar? Or we can bring the tub to your chamber, if ye prefer to bathe."

Considering the possibilities of accepting the offer and having a certain lass joining him, Alex nodded slowly. "I would welcome a good cleansing in my chamber."

Eamon smacked him across the back. "Good. I will

inform a few of the lads to place the wooden tub in your chamber."

Before the man moved around him, Alex halted his progress with an outstretched arm. He swallowed, attempting to speak his mind. "I must discuss an important matter with ye."

The man's eyes narrowed suspiciously. Giving Alex a curt nod, he motioned outward. "Follow me."

Eamon made steady strides away from the castle. Passing through a dense cluster of pines, he led him to a stone bench surrounded by birch trees. He gestured for Alex to take a seat.

"Nae," he waved off dismissively.

The man shrugged. Folding his arms over his chest, Eamon regarded him with a strained expression. "Aine?"

Alex rubbed a hand down the back of his neck to ease the tension. "Aye."

"Should we include Keegan in this conversation?"

Alex laughed nervously and kicked a pinecone out of his path. "And have him take a fist to my face?"

"Explain, MacFhearguis!"

Alex arched a brow. He did not fear the man. He did not fear Keegan. He did not fear the entire Fae kingdom. What Alex feared was the possibility of a life without Aine.

Sighing heavily, he gazed upward. "'Tis quite simple. I love Aine and wish to marry her." He smiled, surprised at his own declaration. When he resumed his focus on the man, he almost laughed at Eamon's expression.

"About bloody time ye came to your senses. Ye are a different man whenever Aine enters a room." Reaching out, Eamon grasped his shoulder. "Here I thought ye

Mary Morgan

were going to confess to bedding my niece. If so, ye would be banished from Taloch."

Alex's heart hammered against his chest. To steer the conversation in another direction, he asked, "Do ye expect Rory at the feast tonight?"

Eamon's good humor vanished. "Unsure."

"Can ye not summon him?"

His eyes widened in alarm. "Summon a Fenian warrior? From the Fae realm? Nae! When the warrior has concluded his time with the other elders, he'll make an appearance."

Frustration clawed at Alex. Would he ever return to Leòmhann?

"Have ye spoken to Aine about your offer? If so, has she accepted?" pressed Eamon, shifting his stance. "Ye do ken many men sought to claim her for a wife. And for reasons she would not divulge, she accepted none."

His hands clenched at the thought of another man taking Aine. "She has not mentioned the others," he admitted slowly. "My purpose was speaking with ye first. Ye are her uncle."

A smile twitched at the corners of Eamon's mouth. "I am honored. Though ye do not need my blessings. I ken ye are an honorable man. Even Rory has spoken of your honor."

Guilt plagued Alex. *Honorable? Would ye still consider me with honor if ye learned I had bedded your niece?*

Eamon wrapped an arm across Alex's shoulders. "Come. Ye must speak with Aine before this day ends. 'Tis one of magic. Furthermore, there is a battle to prepare for, and *ye* play an important part. Then in the afternoon, games to test the warriors' strength."

"Battle?" asked Alex with uneasiness.

The man shook him. "Aye! The one between the Oak King and the aging Holly King."

Alex regarded him skeptically. "Let me guess. I am the *aging* Holly King."

"Of course! And Keegan—"

"Is the Oak King who *slays* me," interjected Alex dryly.

"The battle will be great amusement," encouraged Eamon, releasing his hold on him.

"Definitely for Keegan," grumbled Alex.

Shouting near the castle halted their conversation. Aine came running over the bridge with Etain keeping pace beside her. She showered Alex with a dazzling smile before thrusting a small package into his hands.

"Warm bread and cheese to break your fast," she announced with excitement.

He smiled in return. "My thanks."

An awkward silence hung between them while Eamon maintained his presence next to Alex.

"Eat your meal," she urged, touching his hand with her fingers. "'Tis bread I have made, and a first without a blemish of scorch marks." Pride for her baking spread across her features as she waited for a response from him.

Alex chuckled, eager to taste her fare. He'd gladly devour anything from the lass. "Can I do so in the great hall? Or…" He looked beyond Aine to find her brother advancing on them with rapid strides.

"Ready for the battle, Holly King!" bellowed Keegan, displaying his sword in the air.

"For the love of the Goddess," protested Aine, shaking her head.

"Now?" asked a stunned Alex, watching while others from the castle followed behind the man, each carrying a holly or oak branch.

"Let the man finish his meal before ye condemn him to his death!" she shot back over her shoulder.

Her brother pointed to the newly risen sun with his blade. "First challenge of the day—slay the Holly King and feast with the arrival of the Oak King!"

Alex placed a hand over the hilt of his sword. "Should I be worried?"

"Nae," drawled Eamon, folding his arms over his chest. "However, one can never tell when Keegan judges the rules require changing."

"Often to his advantage," complained Aine, giving her brother a scornful look.

Alex muttered a curse. Unwrapping the bundle in his hand, he took a huge bite of bread and cheese. Shoving the remainder back to Aine, he unsheathed his sword.

Eamon removed the skin attached to his belt. "Here. A swallow of ale before your battle."

Alex coughed, almost choking on his food. He nodded his thanks while taking the offering. After slaking his thirst, he wiped his mouth with the back of his hand and promptly returned the ale skin to Eamon.

Keegan approached and tapped the ground with his blade. "Let this challenge to the death begin near the oak tree by the stream. Time for the reign of the Holly King to end."

A chorus of boisterous voices echoed around them. Eamon waved and shouted for the crowd to follow him along the path to view the battle.

Understanding his demise would be swift, Alex was determined not to die without a good and proper fight.

He gestured outward to Keegan. "Lead the way."

Aine reached for his hand. She gave him a hard squeeze, and then darted a glance at her brother and his group of followers as they ambled toward the stream. "His left arm is the commanding and strongest," she uttered softly. "He will do his best to draw blood from ye."

Touched by her concern, Alex lowered his head near her ear. "Ye can kiss my wounds later."

When he drew back, she rewarded him with a wink before joining the others.

"Will ye walk with me?" he asked, making long strides toward the lass, and passing the lumbering wolfhound who trailed after her.

She looked affronted. "I cannot! This is not your day. Come Midsummer, ye shall reign once again."

"Surely ye can grant a dying man's last request, aye? Or a wish?" he insisted.

Aine stumbled over a slushy patch of snow, giggling. "Ye have an odd request, Holly King. Be careful the *wishes* ye spout on a midwinter day."

When he caught up with her, Alex noted the mirth flashing within her eyes. "Should I make a wish for ye to marry me—the *aging* Holly King?"

Halting her stride, Aine's gaze grew wary. "Ye would offer me marriage? Why would the Holly King make such a request?" Her voice barely a whisper.

Alex reached for her hand, but she took a hesitant step back.

"Why do ye wish to marry?" she demanded with more force.

Keegan's order for Alex to appear bellowed throughout the trees, and Aine snapped her attention over her shoulder.

Determined to get an answer before the mock battle, Alex dropped his sword and brought Aine to his chest. Her hands fisted against his shoulders. "'Tis a simple question," she prodded softly.

His tongue became trapped, unable to free the one word—a word he'd never confessed to another, not even to his brothers. Alex might have told Eamon how he felt for his niece, but it was entirely different spouting the word to the actual person. He swallowed twice.

Her mouth thinned in disapproval. And hurt reflected in her gaze. She struggled to be released, and sadly, Alex complied. Clenching his hands by his side, he watched her retreat back along the path to the castle with her faithful companion by her side.

An ache settled inside him. How could he profess what he felt if she continued to be unsure herself? He'd spend a life doomed by difficulty over one damnable word. Yet a life without Aine left him without breath in his lungs.

Alex blew out a curse and raked a hand through his hair. "I love ye, Aine Fraser!"

The lass froze before the bridge. Slowly turning around, Aine's eyes regarded him for several heartbeats. Dropping the bundle of food in front of Etain, she then gathered up her gown and ran back to him.

Alex caught her in one grasp, bringing her against his chest. "I do love ye," he murmured against her cheek.

"And I love ye, *my warrior*." Cupping his face in her warm hands, she kissed him soundly on the mouth.

A great burst of joy infused Alex with her own confession. His heart soared, and he deepened the kiss. When Keegan's demands raged on, Alex let out a groan and released his hold on Aine. "I fear 'tis time I face the Oak King."

Aine wrapped her arms around his waist with a smile as intimate as their kisses. "Later, I will give ye my answer to your proposal."

He dropped his head against her forehead. "My chamber. After the first round of drinking." Though he'd already guessed her response.

She laughed heartily. "The first and second cups have already been sampled earlier. This is a long day of celebrations." Wiggling free from his embrace, she wandered down toward the stream beyond the trees.

Alex retrieved his sword and followed in a leisurely manner behind her.

By the time he entered the clearing by the stream, the crowd had placed branches of oak in a wide circle. Keegan stood confident in the center, basking in the enjoyment with the others.

Aiming his sword at the man, Alex shouted, "Remember, I will reign come Midsummer."

Keegan's mouth pulled into a sour grin. "Are ye planning on staying at Taloch until the summer?"

Alex shrugged. "Perchance the Gods shall allow me to return here to assert my leadership through the harvest."

The man burst out in laughter. "Ye assume to have favor with them, MacFhearguis? And for the moment, ye are unable to venture *out* of here."

"Are ye on good terms with the Gods that ye would question them?" challenged Alex, stalking toward his foe.

Keegan spread his arms wide. "Most assuredly. Otherwise, they would not grant me this honor."

After removing his tunic, Alex dipped his head slightly when he entered the circle. And the battle began in earnest.

His foe proved to be a worthy challenger. Though the battle was a mock display, Aine's words of warning came thundering into his mind with each blow or a fist to his body. Mindful of each strike of Keegan's blade, he attempted to stay out of thrusting range of the man's sword. Nevertheless, his foe managed to cross his path and slash across his arm with his blade. Though the wound minor, blood pooled forth.

The people cheered, and Alex fought the urge to glare at them.

"Blood is drawn!" shouted Keegan, taunting him from the edge of the circle.

"Mercy for the aging Holly King!" yelled a woman.

"Aye," mumbled an irritated Alex, ignoring the burning sting along his arm.

Wishing to end this folly, Alex dropped to one knee and placed his sword upon the ground. "Hail the Oak King."

A great roar resounded all around him as the people rushed to greet the new king.

Cara scampered over to him. She pressed a sprig of holly against his leather belt. "To let ye ken we shall miss the Holly King. Ye have brought us great joy this harvest."

Alex gazed into her blue eyes which shone brightly in the sunlight. He tapped a finger to the sprig. "I am honored."

Placing her tiny hand over his heart, she whispered, "Do not fear if ye are parted from the one ye love. There is another path that awaits ye."

Speechless to utter a response, Alex frowned.

Cara gave him a beaming smile and darted off to be with the other children.

Rising slowly, Alex's gaze swept the crowd searching for only one woman. His Aine. When his sight rested on her, he whispered, "We shall never be parted, *leannán*. For ye now hold my heart."

Chapter Fifteen

"Do not rejoice over the songbirds' melody. Their tune can either herald joy or impending death." ~Fae Lore

Alex winced, easing the tunic over his bruised shoulders. He hissed out a curse as he straightened from the bed. For a mock battle, Keegan had managed to land numerous blows to certain parts of his body. Briefly, he considered slamming a fist to wipe the smug look of triumph from the man's face. Clearly, the man forgot the rules to this particular fight along with the other games of strength later in the afternoon.

Yet Alex did not want to suffer the wrath of the people who had pledged their praises of victory for the new king. He refrained, barely. Until he managed to land one blow against Keegan's nose. Alex judged the man's features would be marred for some time.

When all the games had concluded, Alex almost shouted in triumph.

Quickly returning to his chamber, he found the tub positioned near the hearth, filled with hot water. A reward for remaining honorable during the battle. So he had been told by Eamon. And Alex took full pleasure for an hour of no interruptions. Until Hamish came bounding into his chamber to announce Glenna was on her way with Aine to deal with his injuries.

And so ended Alex's quiet tranquility.

With the help of the healer, Aine cleansed and bandaged the wound on his arm. Alex hoped he'd have a few moments alone with his *leannán*. But she fled the chamber after leaving him fresh clothing for the evening's feast.

He reached for his belt and wrapped the leather around his tunic. Instinctively, he grabbed his sword from the furs. "Nae. This is a time of feasting."

Smiling, Alex strode with purpose out of the chamber.

While passing a couple of women along the narrow corridor, he smiled. They laughed and dipped a curtsy.

"Nae longer the Holly King," he declared over his shoulder.

"Aye, ye are!" they shouted in unison.

Shaking his head in good humor, Alex maneuvered his way around the corner, and halted his stride. A musical voice floated up the stairway, swirling around him. The woman sang a song of two lovers, each given a quest to prove their love.

Intrigued, Alex descended the stairs. When he reached the entrance of the great hall, his mouth dropped open to gaze at the beauty sitting by a blazing hearth. Her eyes were closed as she plucked the strings of her harp— captivating those within the hall with her siren's song and bardic tale.

"Aine, *my Aine*," he whispered hoarsely.

Alex's heart slammed against his chest. Gone was the beauty usually covered in grime from the forge, and in her place, a woman who rivaled any Goddess. Aine's hair spilled over her shoulders in beautiful curls, cascading over an ivory and golden gown. Firelight pooled behind her, capturing her in its glow. Aine's musical lilt filled the hall with warmth, even beyond the fire snapping behind her.

Stepping inside, Alex nodded to one of the young lads and leaned against the wall. Content to watch from afar, he listened with rapt attention and smiled. His gaze traveled the expanse of the great hall, overflowing with the scent of pine boughs and apples tied with ribbons woven throughout. Fresh rushes graced the floor, and most of the dogs were stretched out by the hearth. Though Etain appeared content to rest at the feet of her mistress.

When Aine had finished, a cheer of approval echoed within the hall. The children rushed forward with their praises, and Etain lifted her large form, stretched, and lumbered over to the other dogs.

"Her voice is beautiful," mentioned Glenna, moving to his side.

"Aye," he agreed, softly. "A voice like none I have heard."

"A rare musical tone—one like her mother. Melvina lured Aine's father, Conan, with her voice of song many years ago."

He glanced sideways at the woman. "Did ye ken the woman?"

"Aye. I knew them both. After Conan brought Melvina to Taloch, I attempted to ease the worry and fear she had for her children. He sought permission from the elders to return, and in a rare decision, they granted his request. However, with each passing year, I grew wary of the woman. Even the elders became concerned by her actions. She'd punish Keegan with a whip if she caught him using any magic."

Alex hissed in disapproval. "And Aine?"

"Fortunately, Aine started to show signs of her growing power after her mother left Taloch."

"What about their father? Why didn't he stop her?" Alex's voice weighed heavy with sarcasm.

Glenna sighed with exasperation. "His love for Melvina blinded him to look beyond and see the real woman who despised what the Fae represented. The old ways."

The thought of anyone beating a child brought a scorching fury inside of Alex. Even his father had spared the whip. Instead, he'd lectured him on the MacFhearguis lineage, and then sent him to serve the stable master and other lads for one week.

"The fight between the old beliefs and the new religion sweeping across the Highlands has many people fearing both," shared Alex quietly.

"'Tis a battle which extends to the Fae realm." Clasping her hands together, she mused, "Good or bad, change is the way forward."

"And after their mother left?" urged Alex, wanting to learn more about Aine's past.

"Conan was a good man and father. Aine adored him and learned her skills within the forge from him," remarked Glenna. "As for Keegan, his story is one that requires patience. He observes—keeps the anger toward his parents hidden away. There is a sadness beneath the banter and sternness. Furthermore, his loyalty to his sister is a bond ye should never attempt to break."

Alex shifted his stance. *I see all of ye, Aine, and I love both.*

"Aine's musical voice could tame even the wildest beast," observed Glenna.

He coughed into his hand to squelch the laughter. Recovering, he said, "Or any hardened warrior?"

This time, Glenna laughed. She touched his arm. "Even the fiercest beast can find comfort in a luring song."

One of the women waved in their direction, and Glenna responded with her own. "Enjoy the feast, Holly King," she teased, making her way across the hall.

Alex watched the woman depart and then resumed his study of Aine. Pushing away from the wall, he made leisurely strides around the tables toward her. Her attentive audience were doing their best to encourage another song. But when she caught his gaze, Aine rose slowly from her chair.

He dipped a slight bow. "I enjoyed your song."

"I am pleased, Holly King." After placing her lap harp on the chair, Aine rested her hand in the crook of his arm.

Sorely tempted to guide his *leannán* out of the hall to spend some time alone with her, he refrained and led Aine to a table where others were engaged in a lively discussion about the morning battle and games of strength.

After settling into her chair, Aine leaned near him. "Ye look magnificent in the dark blue tunic."

Slipping his hand under the table, Alex grasped her fingers. "More clothing from your uncle. And ye are a vision of beauty, my Aine."

Her eyes roamed his features. "I so wanted to please ye tonight."

Alex squeezed her fingers. "Why tonight?"

She covered his hand with her free one. "Because I wanted ye to see the woman and not the lass who likes to fashion blades."

Tilting his head to the side, he commented, "Have I not mentioned, I love both? Ye are soft—yet forged with steel."

Joy bubbled in her laugh and shone in her eyes. She gestured outward. "Did ye taste the bread filled with nuts and honey?"

Alex dropped his hand. "Nae. I have recently arrived."

Quickly tearing a portion of the bread apart, she placed the piece on his trencher. Pointing to the salmon, she nudged him. "The sauce is mixed with rosemary and onions. Rowena even used wild garlic in the turnips."

"Did ye assist in making these tempting fares?" he asked, picking up a blade and spearing a slice of boar.

She snorted, then quickly recovered. "I confess, the kitchens will not be my strength, unless ye ask me to chop vegetables."

"I did enjoy the one bite of bread this morn. And ye did make a tasty porridge the other day," he reminded, taking a bite of the meat.

Two rosy stains appeared on her cheeks. "Aye, a first."

Alex choked on the piece of boar, recalling the pleasurable morning in the gatehouse.

Aine swiftly poured him a cup of mead. "Here," she urged, shoving the cup into his hand.

Grateful for the liquid, Alex proceeded to drain the contents.

Pushing a trencher of cabbages and onions toward him, Aine asked, "Were ye responsible for Keegan's broken nose?"

"I straightened it."

163

"There was nothing wrong with his nose," she retorted, stabbing a piece of fish with a large fork.

"I thought to give him a more pleasing face to court the women," he answered while scooping out a portion of the food into his bowl.

Amusement flickered in the eyes that met his as she placed the fish alongside his vegetables. "Pity I was not there to witness his fall."

"He did not fall," corrected Alex. "I made certain a tree was behind him when I landed the blow to his face."

"Ye do ken he will want payment for your deed." She ripped another piece of bread from the loaf and took a small bite.

Alex chuckled low. "And what kind of payment does your brother prefer?"

Laughter bubbled forth from Aine. She twisted in her chair and tapped his nose with her finger. "He'll want to exact the same to ye."

"Perchance a proper battle in the lists tomorrow morn."

Aine shook her lovely head. "After feasting all night?" Giving Alex a seductive smile, she added, "Nae one wants to greet the new dawn after seeking comfort in the arms of another."

He cleared his throat, pretending not to be affected. "I can assure ye, my strength shall not be an issue after all night bedding ye."

When her mouth dropped open, Alex resisted the urge to capture those rosy lips he cherished.

"Mead?" he suggested, moving the cup toward her.

One of the older men wandered over to their table. He bent and whispered into Aine's ear. As he straightened, a frown marred her features. After receiving a quick nod, the man made his way from the hall.

Concerned, Alex asked, "What did he want?"

Aine pushed her chair back and stood. "My uncle wishes to speak with me."

"Would ye like me to accompany ye?" Rising slowly, he confessed, "I did speak with your uncle about my desire to wed ye."

Her smile returned. "Then I deem this is what he wants to discuss with me."

"I shall walk with ye."

"Nae. Please enjoy the food and drink," she urged. "I intend to make this a short conversation."

Alex dipped his head in agreement. He watched as she wove her way around the tables and vanished from his sight. Other men and women wandered by his table, expressing their esteem for giving them a fine battle this midwinter. He raised his cup in appreciation.

Glancing around the table, Alex determined he didn't want to engage in any further celebrations without his Aine.

Therefore, he left the feasting and boisterous crowd to wait for his beloved in a quieter setting.

Chapter Sixteen

"If ye do not favor the words of your foe, settle the argument by the full moon of midwinter."
~MacFhearguis Motto

When Aine entered her uncle's solar, she regarded him staring out the window. Both shutters had been drawn back, allowing the cold breeze to sweep inside the room. His rigid stance spoke volumes to her. She shivered, but not from the chill within the room. Fear gripped her heart.

"Ye want to speak with me, Uncle?"

He kept his back to her. "Close the door, Aine."

After complying to his request, she padded softly across the room and leaned against the table. A tremor of uncertainty washed over her. Aine's love for Alex meant everything to her. Was her uncle upset over this union? "What is wrong?" she asked in a hushed voice.

Turning to face her, his voice was taut with strain. "I received a message from Rory."

Aine braced her hands on the smooth wood to steady herself. "Are they angry with me? What have the elders decided?"

"Far worse," he announced, tossing the partially rolled parchment onto the table. A small amber crystal attached to a silver chain tumbled forth.

Aine could not fathom the reasoning. Aye, she had

166

gone against everything she had been taught. But she had hoped Rory could make an appeal in her favor. Did she not find love with a man willing to marry and take care of her beyond this haven?

"Read his message," ordered her uncle.

With trembling hands, Aine unfurled the parchment. Her eyes swiftly scanned the written document. Bile rose into her throat, and Aine fought its release. Pressing her fist to her stomach, she continued to read until the last line.

"*Nae!*" The blood pounded in her ears while the room blurred in front of her, pulling her into a dark void.

In two strides, Uncle Eamon rushed to her side and settled her into a nearby chair. "Breathe, Aine," he encouraged softly.

She bent forward, attempting to draw a single breath into her body. Her uncle continued with soothing words to ease her breathing. Finally, Aine lifted her head. Tears smarted her eyes, and she fought hard against spilling them. On a choked sob, she demanded, "Because of my *wishes*, I have endangered Alex's world? Altered those who dwell within Leòmhann?"

Her uncle leaned against the desk. "Aye. With your power, ye altered lives, including the kin of Alex MacFhearguis. Also, the veil is torn, allowing those who we do not want to enter to come through."

Standing abruptly, Aine fought the wave of dizziness. She stumbled over to the window. Her gaze drifted to the twinkling stars, and she pressed a fist against her heart. "And here I thought ye were going to discuss my plans to marry Alex." She laughed bitterly.

"He did ask for my permission," declared Eamon softly.

"Aye, he did mention this to me." The thought of Alex speaking with her uncle first made Aine love him more. "He is good man," she expressed softly.

"Did ye confess all to the man, Aine? Specifically, your lineage?"

A tear slipped down her cheek, and she wiped away the moisture. "Nae," she murmured with regret. "My plans were to tell him tonight."

"Perchance this is good he does not ken about ye and Keegan."

Aine gave her uncle a sharp glance over her shoulder. She disagreed with him. Everything she held dear within her was now shattered. Where moments earlier joy had infused her heart, she now felt adrift on a barge of sorrow to right a wrong.

"Are ye certain I cannot go with him?"

Eamon sighed wearily. "Aye. Without permission, death would claim ye before ye took one step into his Scotland." Her uncle clasped his hands behind his back. "Ye ken what must be done. Only ye can wield the power with the crystal. The veil is already thinning."

Resuming her attention to the stars, Aine steeled her grief. She'd have the rest of her life to mourn her warrior. Tonight, she'd return what was not granted to her. And Cara's earlier words as the Seer slammed with force into her mind.

Her lips trembled. "Aye." Turning around, she went to the table and picked up the amber crystal. Placing the pendant over her neck, Aine battled the emotions swirling in a tempest inside her. Gritting her teeth, she wiped a hand over her brow.

"Would ye like a few moments alone with Alex? To explain what is happening?"

"Nae," she stated with conviction. Understanding her warrior, he'd fight until his last breath to drag her with him to Leòmhann, even if death claimed him.

Picking up the parchment, Aine went to the blazing hearth. Crumbling the message within her hand, she flung it into the fire. She watched as the flames licked a path along the edges of the parchment until they were nothing but ashes. Returning her attention to her uncle, she ordered, "Have anyone but Keegan attend to the horses. I do not want my brother to learn of this until after Alex is gone."

Nodding in understanding, her uncle started forward, but Aine shook her head. Her resolve hardened. Her tone flat. "Do not give me comfort, Uncle Eamon. Once Alex is gone, I shall cry my tears until there are nae more to give."

Heaving a sigh, he turned around and went to the door. His hand stilled on the bolt. "When the day comes for another man to enter—"

"Hear my words—my vow, Uncle," interrupted Aine tersely. "There will *never* be another man. Ever. From this night forward, my life is bound to Taloch. Never shall I venture into Scotland."

Eamon studied her briefly over his shoulder and then quietly left the solar.

Aine shook with fury and grief. Determined to make the last few hours with Alex memorable, she would pour out her heart and final secret to the man. He deserved nothing less. She wiped away another tear that managed to slip down her cheek.

With quick strides, she went to retrieve her cloak and heavier shoes from her chamber. After donning both, Aine went to Alex's chamber. Reaching for his cloak draped over the trunk by his bed, she brought the garment to her face. Inhaling deeply, she committed to memory his scent. Next, she grabbed his sword. Rubbing a finger over the lion carved on the hilt, she whispered, "Courage, my warrior."

Aine clenched her jaw to kill the sob in her throat. She hurried from the chamber and descended the stairs. By the time her foot landed on the bottom step, Aine had steadied her emotions. When she entered the hall, her eyes scanned across the breadth of merry-making.

Hamish darted past her carrying a handful of damson tarts. She managed to grab the lad, bringing him to a sudden halt. "Have ye seen Alex?"

Fruit stains marred his face and hands as he answered, "Nae. Did ye ken Keegan is teaching me to play chess?"

She gave the lad a small smile. "Is he bribing ye with tarts?"

He nodded his head in good humor. "They are his favorite."

Aine placed a kiss along his brow. "Then off with ye, Hamish. Keegan does not like to be kept waiting."

The lad bounded with joy into the hall.

"Where are ye, Alex?" She stood on her tiptoes, searching the hall.

"Is there a reason ye have my cloak and sword, *leannán*?" The burr of the man's question warmed the side of her neck.

Aine turned toward him, giving Alex a beaming smile. "Where have ye been?"

"Watching the numerous stars in the sky out in the bailey."

"I want to show ye a favored spot within the forest,"

she announced, trying to keep her voice calm.

"'Tis cold, Aine, to venture out into a forest this night. What happened with the meeting with your uncle?"

She held out his items. "Once there, ye can keep me warm. The stars are stunning, especially during midwinter. There I'll tell ye about the discussion with my uncle."

His smile sent a stab of pain through her, but Aine turned away and started for the entrance. "I've had our horses made ready," she shot out over her shoulder.

"Ye have thought of everything, *leannán*."

Both horses stood poised and waiting. Beast snorted his usual greeting, and Alex quickly assisted her onto Drust.

"At least there is nae threat of snow," she declared, pulling the hood of her cloak over her head.

Alex cast his sight upward. "The stars are different here." He pointed beyond her. "Are those shaped in the form of a dragon?"

Aine chuckled, releasing some of her anguish. "Aye, *aye*. She represents the Guardians who once roamed Scotland. There are many others. Let me show ye."

Without giving him time to respond, Aine nudged her horse forward into a gallop over the bridge, leading Alex toward the great forest. Onward they traveled across the snow-covered land. When the forest loomed ahead of them, Aine slowed Drust's pace. As they neared, she swiftly dismounted.

Leaning near the animal, she whispered, "Etain has revealed the path to us. Therefore, ye must show Beast to the edge of the veil. He has to go on through with Alex."

Drust's ears pricked up, and he let out an unpleasant snort. Clearly, he thought her plan unwise.

"Do not fail us," she prodded softly. "Many lives depend on us, my friend."

Aine swept a glance over her shoulder to make sure Alex followed her lead. Giving a tug on the reins, she urged the horse forward.

"Are ye certain we need to walk through a forest to look at the stars?" complained Alex.

Ignoring his concerns, Aine trudged upward along the narrow path. With each step, her heart splintered more. Making slow and steady strides, she paused every few moments to make sure Alex remained behind her. Her heart hammered fiercely with each step she took toward their destination. Bending low, she swept aside the branches to allow her horse and Alex to enter the small clearing at the top.

"The stars are stunning, but I sense ye are troubled, *leannán*."

After dropping Drust's reins, Aine went to the exact spot where she saw Alex for the first time. As her body began to quake, she drew in a shaky breath and released it slowly in an attempt to keep her voice calm. "Where we stand is sacred ground, especially to the Fae. There is something I need to tell ye, Alex, and I needed to bring ye here. 'Tis one more secret I have held back."

Worry creased his brow as he approached. Placing his hands on her shoulders, she felt his strength seep into her. "Tell me."

She licked her lips, uncertain how to proceed.

He lifted her chin with his finger. "Nothing ye say will change how I feel about ye, Aine. I love ye. Always."

Sighing heavily, Aine blurted out, "My father was kin to the Fae King Ansgar. He is a distant cousin. Making Keegan and me belonging to—"

"*Royalty*," interrupted Alex in a stunned tone.

Alex drew back and scrubbed a hand over his face. Silence reigned between them like an unwelcomed companion while she watched him stare upward.

Aine fought the misery and moved closer to the veil opening. Courage and determination were like a rock inside her. She clutched the amber crystal. The power burned through her palm and seared up her arm. "Are ye angry with me for not telling ye sooner?"

He crossed the distance to her in two strides. Grasping Aine around the waist, his gaze bore into hers. "I give nae regard if ye are the Queen of the Fae. I love ye, Aine Fraser. And ye are going to be my wife! Are ye telling me I have to ask *your* king's permission to marry ye?"

"Nae," she answered feebly, burying her face against his chest. "But my discussion with my uncle is one ye need to hear."

"I am listening, *my leannán*."

Shrugging out of his grasp, Aine neared the entrance between their worlds. The air thinned. She noted Drust leading Alex's horse to the opening.

Lifting her head to the stars, her voice turned reflective. "When I started making wishes many moons ago, I never imagined my heart opening to love. I simply wanted to venture out to your Scotland." Tears pooled against her lashes, finally spilling down her cheek.

Aine returned her attention to the man who held her heart. "I will love ye always, my warrior—*my champion*." She swiped away the moisture on her face before continuing, "Now 'tis time for the lion of Leòmhann to return to his clan. Alone."

A dark cloud settled over Alex's features. He stormed to her side. "What are ye saying?"

"When I made my last wish and ye came through, the veil became torn. In using magic to split the veil, I altered the lives of those who ye hold dear. Your kin. Time shifted. Battles will be fought, and deaths shall follow. This midwinter night, ye have to return—to mend the rift in the veil," she pleaded.

"Not without ye," he growled, clenching his fists by his sides.

Her voice wavered. "I am not permitted. If ye attempt to take me through, my death shall be swift."

"Nae, *nae!*" he thundered. "I cannot live a life without ye!"

"Would ye doom the life of your kin? For our happiness?" she uttered softly.

Uncertainty flickered within his eyes.

"Ye are their chieftain—to protect and defend."

"Do not remind me of my responsibility! Often a burden I have fought daily," he argued.

"But your heart is your clan, Alex. Ye would die for them."

"I would *die* for ye!"

Aine touched his lips with her fingers to silence his protests. "We have known love. Let this brief time together carry us through our darkest moments. Ye must go *now*," she urged. "Save your people."

He hissed out a curse and grabbed her arms. "Aye, my duty belongs to my clan." His voice resigned. "But my heart will always be with ye."

Alex covered her mouth. His kiss became urgent—

demanding, and Aine surrendered one last time. Slowly, he drew away from her, and she steeled her heart in anticipation.

Removing the crystal pendant from beneath her cloak, she spoke the opening words to send Alex through. "From this world, to the next—"

"Stop!" implored Alex. "There has to be a way to undo what happened! To prevent any harm to my clan! Can ye not speak with Rory?"

The wind lashed around them in an angry uproar along with Alex's pleas.

Aine stepped to the side. Allowing the power of the crystal to fill her, she lifted her voice outward. "From the four quarters of both realms—east, south, north, and west, hear my request, mighty Guardians. Grant me the power once more to bend the veils between the realms. To right a wrong and send this warrior back home."

The ground rumbled beneath them, but her resolve strengthened by the power she held, and the sacrifice required to heal the rift.

"*Aine, nae!*" bellowed Alex, reaching out to her in a final plea and attempt to halt her actions. Yet the power pulled him onward through the opening.

In desperation, her hand lifted toward his fading body. "Remember our love, Alex! I will love ye until the stars are nae more!"

With a resounding clap of thunder, her warrior vanished from her sight, and Aine collapsed onto the ground in tormenting agony. His last anguished cry slashed at her heart like a thousand blades. She yanked the crystal off from around her neck and tossed it outward. As she knelt on the ground, Aine lifted her tearful sight to the stars.

Unable to contain her sorrow any longer, a loud, mournful cry ripped free from her throat.

Chapter Seventeen

"Without love, the heart ceases to beat, becoming trapped in a shell of unrelenting torment." ~Fae Lore

Fighting the agonizing pain searing into his head, Alex attempted to force air into his starving lungs. He breathed in shallow, quick gasps. On a groan, he rolled to the side and emptied what little he had in his gut. Powerless to stand, he scooped up a handful of snow and wiped the icy mixture over his face. The coldness eased the burning inside his head. With great effort, he moved to a sitting position.

A wet muzzle nudged his ear. Cracking open his eyes, Alex surveyed his surroundings. Beast hovered over him, twitching his tail. "Help me to stand," he requested hoarsely.

After taking the reins, and with the help of his horse, Alex managed to gain his feet. He rubbed a hand over his animal's dark mane and looked beyond their position.

Gone was the path he stepped through weeks ago by the oak trees during the heavy snowfall. He'd been drawn to the area by the shimmer in the mists surrounding lush foliage without any traces of snow. Yet now the trees were as barren and devoid of any light and warmth. Gray clouds fought what little sunlight streaked within the sky, adding more to his misery.

Alex stumbled over to one of the trees. Numbing

sorrow filled him. He rubbed the heel of his palm across his heart to ease the unbearable grief coursing throughout him. The Gods had struck a mallet straight into his heart, and the brutal torment of loss left him without breath. Raw grief consumed him.

His beloved was gone.

In a rage, he slammed his fist against the aging giant. "Aine!" he bellowed, the sound echoing around him.

Footsteps resounded behind him. In one swift move, Alex unsheathed his sword and faced the intruder.

"Alex?" shouted Patrick, making long strides to him. "By the Gods, I am relieved to find ye!" As he approached, a look of wariness creased his features. "Why have ye not returned to Leòmhann? Did ye want to spend three days alone—"

"*Three days*," interjected Alex in disbelief.

A slight hesitation shone in his brother's hawklike eyes. "Aye, though why are ye wearing that tunic? 'Tis not the one ye had on when ye departed the hall."

Alex sheathed his blade and leaned against the tree for support. He laughed bitterly. "I had been attending a feast."

Patrick studied him. "In this remote area? Where there are nae others?"

Frustration seethed inside Alex. He turned from his brother's censure and walked forward. Slowly, he parted the bare limbs of one of the oak trees. No path greeted him. No lavender eyes to show him love. Never again would he hold his *leannán* in his arms. Even now, her scent lingered on his cloak.

"Alex, what has happened to ye?" demanded Patrick.

With a heavy sigh, Alex retreated back. He reached

for the reins of his horse. "All is well at Leòmhann? Gwen? Your bairn?"

Patrick blocked their path. "One of the young lads broke his finger engaging in a mock battle on one of the tables in the great hall, but aye, we are well."

Lifting his hand upward, Alex remarked, "The snows have been heavy here."

"Lugh's balls! Most of Leòmhann has been searching for ye." Concern filled his brother's voice.

Worry creased Alex's brow. Nodding slowly, he confessed, "I shall give ye my full account once we have returned to Leòmhann."

Patrick shoved a hand through his hair. "Can ye tell me anything now?"

Quickly mounting his horse, Alex fought the wave of pain overtaking his body again. "I can confess that ye have *lost* our bargain, Patrick. Indeed, I found love." Solemnly, he glanced over his shoulder at the oak trees, adding, "And my wife."

Giving a hard nudge to Beast, he urged the horse onward down the mountain, leaving a dazed Patrick standing all alone.

When the tower of Leòmhann came into view, Alex hardened his despair. *Ye should be beside me, Aine. In an awful twist of Fae fate, our future has been shattered.*

Beast galloped with a sense of fury, matching Alex's. The wind slashed across his face, and his cloak snapped behind him.

When the bridge leading through the portcullis loomed ahead, a great shout rang out from a guard in the gatehouse. They managed to raise the gate in time as both rider and horse raced on through.

People rushed out of the castle and bailey—from

young to old—hailing their chieftain. Some shouted their greetings, and a couple of the women touched Alex on the arm. The stable lad dashed over and offered to escort Beast to the stables for care. One of his guards pressed a cup into his hands, and Alex nodded his appreciation. He downed the ale in several swallows.

Wiping his mouth with the back of his hand, Alex returned the cup to the man. His guarded look eased slightly. *Ye were correct, my leannán.* His duty belonged here with his clan. A responsibility he never wanted, yet a mantle he could no longer shove aside.

His gaze searched beyond the crowd, seeking another woman. When his sight landed on Gwen and the bairn in her arms, Alex believed the future of Leòmhann depended on the descendants of Patrick and his wife. Before he vanished through the veil, Alex made an oath he'd never take another woman.

Gwen moved through the crowd. After brushing off the snow from his cloak, she tilted her head to the side. "I'll have food and drink brought to your chamber. Unless ye prefer to eat in the great hall?"

Alex touched a finger down the cheek of her son. The bairn rewarded him with a smile. His heart clenched. "My chamber," he said softly.

Stepping aside, Alex made long strides into the castle and hurriedly rushed up the narrow stairs to his chamber. Once there, he slammed the door behind him. Darkness greeted him. After ridding his cloak, he strode to the shutters and flung them back. An icy blast of wind blew past him, filling the room.

Fisting his hands on his hips, he stared across the mountaintops, heavy with snow. Deep loneliness, mingled with sorrow, consumed Alex. Would he ever find peace again?

"Nae," he muttered into the quiet stillness.

When the door to his chamber opened, Alex maintained his gaze outward. "Ye can leave the trencher on the table."

"I thought to join ye, Brother."

He glanced sharply at the man. "I prefer to be alone."

"And I disagree. I've brought ale. Food is arriving shortly."

Alex grunted a response.

"By the hounds, are ye with fever? 'Tis cold enough to freeze the balls off any man or beast," complained Patrick.

Ignoring his brother, Alex resumed his silence and gazed toward the land.

"Aye, let me tend to the fire in the hearth to take the chill from your chamber," mocked Patrick, doing his best to dump the wood loudly into the cold hearth.

Pinching the bridge of his nose, Alex tried to temper the yearning to kick his brother out of the chamber.

The crackling of flames came to life behind him, but he continued to glare outward.

When Gwen entered, he finally turned around. She placed a large trencher with stew, bread, and two bowls on the table. After she picked up his discarded cloak from the floor, she placed the garment on top of his trunk by the bed.

Giving him a smile, she suggested, "Try to eat something. Ye look like ye have suffered an ordeal."

Did the woman see beyond his hardness? "My thanks, Gwen."

Patrick reached for her hand before she departed. He

placed a kiss along her knuckles. "Do not wait for me. Go break your fast."

After she left, Patrick dragged another chair to the table near the hearth.

Alex wandered over to his brother's side. He settled into his chair and leaned his forearms on the table. The aroma of food assaulted him, and his stomach growled in protest. "Venison stew?"

"Tessa has been tending to your favorite meal over the fire since ye left." His brother divided the stew into two empty bowls.

He grunted a response before digging into his meal. Thankfully, Patrick remained quiet as he tore into the bread. Grateful for the silence, Alex managed to eat all of the stew. Between the fire's heat and the warm meal, the tension and chill eased from his body.

Filling their cups with ale, Patrick then settled back in his chair and stretched out his legs.

Swirling the liquid within his cup, Alex sighed heavily. "Have I mentioned how much I loathe the meddling of the Fae?"

His brother studied him over the rim of his cup. "Numerous times."

Alex's hand clenched. "For the first time in my life, I found a woman to love." He pounded his fist against his chest. "I loved her!"

"After three days?" Patrick's question laced with skepticism.

Slamming his cup onto the table, Alex pointed a finger at his brother. "Three days to ye, aye. But I have been gone much longer."

The man's eyes narrowed. "How *long*?"

"I celebrated midwinter."

His brother stood abruptly, sending his chair crashing to the floor behind him. "By the Gods," he uttered in a strangled voice. "'Tis weeks before midwinter. Where have ye been?"

Alex motioned for his brother to sit. Once Patrick resumed his position, he flexed his fingers and then crossed his arms over his chest. "Allow me to give my account. Then ye can ask your questions."

Patrick gave a curt nod of approval.

For the next hour, Alex retold his journey into a land shrouded in secrecy within the Great Glen. From his loss of memories, meeting with Rory MacGregor, and finally, falling in love with Aine. The first time he uttered her name aloud in the chamber, he had to pause. He found his voice taut with strain, and the grief of loss surrounded him, reminding Alex of what he could never have.

My leannán.

When he'd recounted everything, Alex sighed wearily. Rising from his chair, he crossed the chamber to the arched window.

Patrick approached and placed a firm hand on his shoulder. "This is not finished, Brother."

Uncertain by his brother's words, he prodded, "Explain."

"The Fae are overdue in granting us our favor," he retorted in disdain. "Do ye not recall the words from the Fenian warriors after the great battle?"

Alex smiled knowingly. Hope flared inside him like sunlight on a summer day. "Ye are correct. The Fae owe the MacFhearguis clan. And I plan to obtain what is due. Why didn't I remember?"

His brother laughed. "Love can perplex the mind to

183

any rational thought."

Glancing outward, he allowed the seed of hope to settle inside his heart. "I shall *demand* the return of my Aine."

****

Midwinter's Eve

"I am sorry, Alex. The weavers from the nearby village have been unsuccessful in contacting anyone from the Fae at the sacred well. They are hopeful their requests will be heard on midwinter," admitted Gwen sadly. "I do understand this doesn't lessen your frustration."

Alex frowned. "Have them abandon their plans. They should be with their kin. And a storm is brewing in the north."

Unrest plagued Alex as he paced within his solar. As the weeks bled on, their pleas to any Fenian warrior went unanswered. Even with the appearance of the Dragon Knights at Leòmhann, not one Fae warrior entered their lands.

He halted his steps when Patrick entered. "How are our guests?"

"Enjoying the mead, giving their advice on the stables, which require additional room—"

"Alastair," interrupted Alex dryly. Leaning against his desk, he shook his head.

His brother's eyes widened in mirth as he crossed to Gwen's side. "Ye ken that Dragon Knight well. He stated the wall needs to be expanded south."

"Alastair MacKay complains and argues about any progress we make at Leòmhann."

"Because he oversaw much of the building of their new castle, Aonach," added Patrick.

184

Alex grunted a curse.

Patrick touched his wife's cheek. "Our son's screams are threatening to bring down the stones in the great hall. 'Tis time for his feeding."

Gwen clucked her tongue in obvious disapproval. "He wails because he wants attention."

His brother looked affronted. "Angus took to holding him and then placed him back in his basket when he let out a wail of protest."

"What if our son saw the dragon's fire within Angus' eyes? Did ye not consider he was frightened?" challenged Gwen.

Patrick arched a brow. "A MacFhearguis *never* fears a Dragon Knight, specifically a MacKay. Let us go tend to our son."

They continued with their conversation while they departed the solar.

Alex leaned against his desk. The lineage in this time was now secured. He need not fear in obtaining an heir.

But this did nothing to banish the daily anguish he suffered. Even mead or ale did nothing to dull his pain. And with each passing day, his temper rose quickly. His mood so foul, the animals scurried out of his way within the bailey. He pressed his hands around the edges of the table.

"Does a MacFhearguis *fear* the Fae?" asked the man standing at the entrance to his solar.

Alex snarled, snapping his gaze to the leader of the Dragon Knights. "Nae!"

A shadow of annoyance crossed the man's face. "Then summon a Fae. Did ye not say ye have been dealing with one of the MacGregors?"

"Aye, Rory MacGregor," admitted Alex, shoving away from the desk. "I have attempted to summon him daily. Even the local weavers loyal to the Fae have been unsuccessful in obtaining any response."

Angus MacKay moved inside the solar with long, purposeful strides. He went directly to the fire. "Would ye care for my assistance?"

Narrowing his eyes, Alex approached the man. "If I cannot get the MacGregor to listen to my request, then what makes ye believe he will answer yours?"

The power of the great fire dragon blazed within Angus' eyes. Withdrawing a small piece of folded parchment from within his belt, he held it outward. "These are the ancient words to summon a Fenian Fae warrior. Hail the warrior at dawn on midwinter."

Clutching the parchment into his hand, Alex asked, "Are ye certain? Only ye contain the power of the dragon who dwells within ye."

Angus chuckled low. "Most assuredly. Since ye are kin to the Dragon Knights, I reckon ye should have the wisdom. But take with ye a symbol of magic from Leòmhann when ye make your demands."

With a renewed sense of determination, Alex smiled broadly at the man.

Chapter Eighteen

Taloch ~ Many weeks after midwinter

Even with the fierce wind whipping around her, Aine continued to rub her thumb over the hilt of the dagger she'd made for Alex. The elements would not sway her with this final task.

In her quest to banish the sorrow, she'd finally completed the dirk. A small part of her wanted to melt the steel and fashion something else—to rid any traces of Alex's time here. However, the quiet solitude in the forge helped her to forget the pain, if only for a few hours. After she'd completed her task yesterday, Aine had lifted the blade to the first light of dawn. Deep sorrow consumed her again.

Within the stillness of each night, her dreams were fraught searching for Alex. And when the dawn arrived, Aine struggled to start the new day.

"Will this torment ever leave my heart?" she shouted into the wind.

Grief and fury—each battling for control.

She looked down at the dirk. Why had she chosen to carve a falcon around the wooden hilt? Why not a lion? Or what about a dragon? None appealed to her, except the wisdom of the falcon.

Tracing her finger over the bird's wings, her tears began anew. "Enough!" She wiped away the annoying moisture.

Etain growled her own complaints by her side.

Aine glanced down at her loyal and steadfast companion. "Ye did not need to accompany me to this dreadful place. I could have managed on my own."

The wolfhound stared mournfully at her.

Aine brushed her fingers over the animal's coarse fur. "I ken ye miss him as well. But he is not returning to us—to me."

She resumed her sight outward. The trees mocked her, daring her to raise her voice with magic. Snow swirled around her in soft flakes, and the scene in front of her blurred.

Aine closed her eyes tightly. "Nae more tears. Not here. Once my quest is complete, I shall never return."

"Why do ye insist on tormenting yourself?" demanded her brother from behind her.

Ignoring his scornful question, Aine opened her eyes and moved to where she'd last seen Alex depart into his world. Even her brother's ranting could not deter her task.

"Storm is coming. Return home," he insisted with more force.

"Home?" Fury sparked her words. Pointing the dirk toward the trees, she snapped, "There was my home! With Alex!"

"Ye were wrong in splitting the veil," he argued, glaring at her. "And Taloch is your home."

How could her brother possibly understand? She had no desire to stand here and debate her reasonings with him.

"Do not remind me of my actions," she warned. "I shall always love Alex. Until ye find love, Keegan, do not speak to me of pain and torment."

Keegan's cloak flapped angrily around his body. "*Love* is not in my future. I will neither welcome nor give the wretched emotion."

Saddened by his declaration, she opened her mouth to ask why he'd forsaken love. Did he glimpse into his future using magic? Or were their parents to blame? Aine snapped her mouth closed and looked beyond him.

"Return to Taloch with me," he urged more softly. "I give ye my vow never to speak harsh words about what has befallen."

Aine smiled sadly at him. "Vow? A first for ye, Keegan."

He held out his hand. "Whatever it takes to see ye happy."

Regardless of his oath, Aine deemed happiness would never enter her heart again.

She glanced down at the dirk in her hands. Bringing the blade to her lips, Aine pressed a kissed along the hilt. "Forever, my warrior."

With careful steps, she went to the largest oak tree. After bending down on one knee, Aine shoved the dirk into the ground with all her might. All that remained visible was the hilt. Rising slowly, Aine tapped the ancient tree sacred to her people. "May the wisdom of the falcon always guide my warrior in his world. Watch over and protect him."

Drawing the hood of her cloak over her head, Aine turned to her brother. "Take me home, Keegan."

****

Leòmhann Castle ~ Midwinter morning

Alex clutched the scrap of parchment in his fist after committing to memory the ancient words written by

Angus. Sunlight streaked across the early morning sky. He honored the midwinter with a silent prayer for this day and to grant his wish. He shoved the parchment inside the belt around his waist and removed the single white rose from Leòmhann. Before he'd departed, he noted the first bud had burst forth. Until the arrival of Gwen, the roses failed to bloom at midwinter. Alex sought to appease the Fae who guarded the oak trees with his token, even if a Fae warrior did not appear.

Bending down on one knee, Alex placed the rose near the base of the largest tree. Rising, he stretched his arms outward, letting the ancient words flow out of him.

"Ye who came from the stars tracing a path along the land, I call ye forth. Open the door to the past, present, and the time yet to come. Stand at the gateway of all tomorrows and bind with me on this sacred site. From my blood to the blood of the Fae, hear me! I call ye forth, Fenian warrior, Rory MacGregor!"

The mists descended, snaking a path through the trees and shrouding the land around Alex. His body pulsed with the words he'd dared to speak aloud, and his breathing became labored, fighting the growing sense of urgency.

"I, Alex MacFhearguis, Chieftain of Leòmhann, call ye forth, Rory MacGregor!" His demand echoed upward. The ground rumbled beneath him, and Alex shifted his stance to maintain control.

Instantly, the mists parted, and Rory stormed through. "Ye dare to command my presence using my name with hallowed and binding words!"

Alex battled with placing his hand over the hilt of his sword. "Ye have ignored my requests for weeks. Ye have *ignored* the pleas from others. I did what had to be done."

Rory's expression turned thunderous. "Where did ye come upon the knowledge to command a Fae warrior?"

Alex crossed his arms over his chest. He did not fear this warrior. Tempering his own anger, he replied, "I did not ken I commanded ye. I sent forth a request for an audience."

"Tread carefully, MacFhearguis, for ye walk a path that could send ye into the abyss." A sudden thin chill hung on the edge of his words.

Alex snorted in disgust. "I have traveled on that dark road."

Rory bit out a curse and clasped his hands behind his back. "What do ye want to discuss?"

"The Fae owe the MacFhearguis clan a favor at a time of our choosing."

The Fae warrior shrugged. "Why?"

"For taking Adam."

Rory flicked a piece of snow from his royal tunic. "Your brother was destined to become a Dragon Knight."

"For the death of Michael," continued Alex.

"Your older brother succumbed to his weakness for power."

"I wish to marry Aine!"

Arching a brow, Rory conceded, "A legitimate reason. But unacceptable."

"Why?" roared Alex. He dared to take a step near the Fae. "Ye who have suffered the agony of being torn apart from the woman ye love would *deny* my request?"

Rory's eyes flashed in outrage. "Ye ken nothing of my torment!"

"And ye ken mine?" challenged Alex. "Ye were given a second chance. I have heard the tales given by the druids. Are the Fae now above their own laws?"

"Be careful the next words ye spout, MacFhearguis," snapped Rory.

Desperation tightened Alex's throat. "I live with this consuming grief that plagues my waking days and nights. Grant me this one request—my wish to have Aine as my wife. To rule Leòmhann with her by my side."

Rory's mouth twisted into a sour grin. "Ye, who have *cursed* the Fae, now desire to claim a woman who is kin to the Fae King?"

Alex laughed, releasing some of his tension. "An interesting predicament, aye. Yet Aine stole my heart the moment I stepped through the trees into her world. I saw beyond the grime of the Fae lass working in a forge to the woman destined to become my wife. I *love* Aine."

When silence lingered between them, Alex tossed out one final plea to the Fae. "If ye will not consider my request—"

"Sounds more like a demand," interrupted Rory, dryly.

Alex continued, "Then allow me to speak with your king."

Unclasping his hands, Rory leaned back and roared with laughter. Quickly recovering, he replied, "Will not happen. Ever. However…"

Rory moved around Alex and went to the oak tree. He placed his palm on the rough bark. "Ye have honored this land, MacFhearguis, as does your brother, Adam. Since this day is sacred to our Fae, the request has already been granted to another. I prodded ye to see how far ye would go to profess your love. Ye might have stated ye loved Aine in the beginning of our conversation."

Stunned, Alex took a hesitant step back. "What are ye saying?"

The Fae warrior stepped aside. He blew across the palm of his hand, and the mists parted between the trees. "With the Fae's blessing, Aine Fraser may enter your world."

A vision of beauty walked toward Alex. A woman he thought to never see again, and his world shifted beneath him.

"Aine, *leannán*." He choked on the words, his throat tight with emotion. His hands trembled as he reached out to her. "Are ye real?"

She rushed into his waiting embrace. "Alex, *Alex*," she murmured his name against his lips. "I am as real as my love for ye."

His emotions whirled and skidded as he took fierce possession of her mouth. The kiss sang through his veins, healing the pain of loss within his heart. Her scent filled Alex, banishing all the sorrow. His mouth grazed her earlobe. "I love ye, *my leannán*. I never wish to be parted from ye again."

A gruff sound intruded behind them.

Without releasing his hold on his beloved, Alex raised his head to find Keegan and Eamon standing within the parted mists. Etain trotted around them, settling near Alex and Aine.

"I am entrusting the care of my sister into your clan, MacFhearguis," stated her brother. "Do not make me regret my actions this day by bringing her sorrow or harm."

Alex loosened his hold on Aine and started forward.

Keegan held up his hand to stay his movements. "'Tis not permitted for ye to cross over, nor are we granted passage into your world. We merely wished to escort Aine safely through the veil along with Etain. The wolfhound would not do well without her mistress."

Giving both men a curt nod, he stated, "My thanks, Keegan and Eamon." Glancing at Aine, he added, "I shall love and cherish your sister and niece always. My sword to defend, my shield to protect, my heart to give her love all the days of her life."

Aine moved into him and gently touched his cheek with her fingers. "My strength shall be yours when storm clouds threaten ye. My touch to banish the darkness from your mind, and the love of my soul until the stars fade from the night sky. Evermore, I am yours."

"Then by the declarations ye both have made and witnessed by us and the Fae warrior, ye are bound in the sacred oath of marriage," announced Eamon.

Rory stepped forth. "Agreed. Ye are now married in the laws of the Fae. Yet there is one condition I have to present to ye before this union is completed."

Alex regarded the Fae. Whatever his condition, he'd gladly accept. Whatever the price, he'd give willingly. Aine would never be parted from him. "State your terms."

Withdrawing a rolled parchment from within his cloak, Rory held it outward to Alex. "An agreement to help govern Taloch, alongside Keegan. With your aid, we can make additional progress on the castle and surrounding lands."

His brow furrowed in confusion. Hesitantly, Alex accepted the document. "Why me?"

Rory smirked. "Why not the lion who braved

another realm to rescue a falcon?"

Aine gasped. "Are ye saying…"

The Fae gazed down at her. "Aye. Ye are his falcon who guided him into your world. The Fates decreed this union thousands of years ago. Nevertheless, the veil became torn. An occurrence that was not foretold. The rift had to be mended in order for your love to find a way back through."

Alex fought the urge to strike out with a few harsh words. *Meddling Fae.* He chuckled softly. "I accept the new position."

"Good!" shouted Keegan. "Ye can return at Midsummer, Holly King! Farewell, Sister! Until summer, may the light of the Fae surround ye."

"May the light of the Gods and Goddesses surround ye, Brother and Uncle Eamon," she returned.

"Then I will alert the Fae elders." Rory paused by the entrance to Taloch. "Prince Conn and my brother, Liam, send their regards. Ye can expect a visit from them when ye arrive at Midsummer."

Groaning, Alex nodded slowly.

Laughter bubbled forth from Aine, and he gave her a warning look.

In a shimmer of brilliant lights, they watched as Keegan, Eamon, and Rory vanished through the trees.

Alex cupped her chin and gazed into his beloved's jeweled eyes. "Then we are married."

When Aine smiled, a shaft of sunlight pierced through the gray clouds over them. Standing on her tiptoes, she whispered, "Although, I would like to have a druid bless our wedding at Leòmhann."

He roared with laughter. "Did ye request another *wish*, my *leannán*?"

Aine linked her fingers with his and placed their joined hands against her heart. "Nae. Simply a request for a marriage in your world."

"*Our* world," Alex corrected while recapturing her mouth in a soul-searing kiss.

Epilogue

Leòmhann Castle ~ Late January 1211

Alex stroked his fingers down the side of his wife's soft breast. "Are ye certain ye do not want to move to the bed?"

She moaned. Wrapping an arm over his chest, Aine snuggled closer to him. "And for the third time, aye. I enjoy lying on the furs in front of the fire with ye." She teased her hand across his stomach, and then stilled her movements. "I can view the stars from this vantage."

He let out a hiss as his cock swelled once again.

Continuing with his pleasurable assault over her skin, he offered, "I could have the bed moved to face the window, my wife."

Aine rested her chin on his chest. "Now?"

A smile tipped the corners of his mouth. "If ye so wish."

Giving him a pout, she objected, "I told ye, I am done making wishes. And I consider it wiser for your men to get their sleep. Between the demands of all the visitors and feasting these past few weeks, 'tis a wonder any of us found rest."

Sighing, he recalled, "I thought the Dragon Knights would never leave."

"Would ye have sent them outward into fierce weather? Nae," she scolded.

"I grew weary of giving the many accounts of the mock battle with your brother—"

"Especially when Alastair stood on the longest table in the great hall and demanded ye show him blow by blow." Aine tried to hide her mirth but failed miserably.

Alex narrowed his eyes. "Most likely the man had consumed too much mead."

"Nae, nae, he did not. He only had the two cups," admitted Aine. "I enjoyed spending time with the men and their wives. It was a great honor to finally meet them, and the clan to witness our second wedding. Gwen and I agreed—"

"By the hounds!" His eyes widened in alarm. "Nae! Do not tell me ye and Patrick's wife have offered to have them visit again. With the wailing bairns, power bursting forth from a few of the young lads, and the constant debate over the best mead…" Alex shook his head. "Again, I say, *nae*."

"Are ye finished, *my chieftain*?"

"Well, aye."

"If ye had let me finish, I was going to mention, Gwen made an offer to include the wives and me in a new group of weavers during the warmer months." Aine splayed her fingers through the hair on his chest. "Sadly, my attempts in the kitchen are poorly, and I deem weaving could be something I might be able to do. For ye."

The tension in his shoulders eased. "Aine MacFhearguis, ye please me by waking each morn within my arms—from the smile that graces your features to the sounds ye make when I am giving ye pleasure."

Two rosy stains blossomed on his wife's cheeks.

"When ye touch my body, I find I am unable to be silent."

"And when ye scream, I shall enjoy capturing your sweet sounds with my mouth." Alex tugged on a curl, adding, "Did I not give ye permission to work in the forge? I am still waiting for the dirk ye promised to make for me."

Aine shifted away from him and drew herself into a sitting position. Her gaze lingered on the flames within the heart. "Alas, I did fashion a dirk for ye."

Frowning, he asked softly, "What happened to the blade? Did ye consider melting the steel down after ye were done?"

She grimaced and bit her lower lip. "Almost. I did finish your dirk during the sorrowful days after ye left. Did ye ken I carved a falcon along the hilt? The blade was my best work."

Alex resisted the urge to bring her back against him. He understood her anguish well. "What did ye do with the dirk, *leannán*?"

Her smile turned melancholy. "I buried the blade into the ground at the exact spot I last saw ye depart. If I had not seen the white stag on my journey back to Taloch, I believe I would have given up and not demanded a meeting with Rory. If the elder had not appeared, I would have requested an audience with the king."

Turning onto his side, his hand reached out to hers. He tugged gently on her fingers, and Aine fell back into his arms. "Tell me again about this rare stag," urged Alex while cradling her warm body.

Aine chuckled softly. "Long ago in the Great Glen on a midwinter twilight, a young woman was returning to her home after visiting with kin. While snow fell heavily around her, she kept moving forward with determination. However, on her path she came upon a white stag trapped in a snowdrift. With the day slipping into darkness, the woman feared if she remained to help the stag, she'd never see the path that would lead her back home. But in her heart, the woman relented. How could she leave another to die in agony? After removing her cloak, she draped the garment over the back of the animal. With nothing but her hands, and whispering prayers to the Fae, the woman managed to free the white stag."

Lifting her head, Aine's eyes glittered in the soft firelight as she continued with her tale. "And when the woman stepped back, the white stag transformed into a man. Grateful for her warmth, prayers, *and* for freeing him, the man pledged his undying love to her. So Fae legend proclaims, if ye are fortunate to see a white stag wandering through the forest on a winter twilight, then true love shall be granted to ye, if ye so wish."

Alex's heart clenched at the possibility of losing Aine again. Swiftly banishing the unwelcomed thought, he sought to dwell on the beauty within his arms. "Your uncle confided to me about the other men offering marriage to ye. Why didn't ye accept?" he asked.

Taking his hand, Aine placed it over her heart. "None stirred me here—inside my heart and soul. I wanted *love*."

For reasons Alex could not fathom, the Fae considered him worthy of this woman. He, a dark and brooding man, was given a rare gift.

After brushing aside a lock of hair from his forehead, she pressed her lips gently over his furrowed brow. "Do not fear, I am not going anywhere without my champion."

He laughed softly. "Ye saved me, Aine. Rescued me from a barren life filled with bitterness. I do not deserve ye but shall strive to be a good husband."

Her smile was as intimate as a kiss. "I never imagined a love so powerful. Each day, I love ye more. And ye are wrong, Alex, ye are worthy of love—*my love*."

"My *leannán*, my *Aine*. I love ye." Alex breathed the words against her lips.

"Show me," she challenged in a silky voice.

Swiftly rolling his beloved onto her back, Alex nudged her thighs apart with his knee. "Where shall I begin?"

Uttering a low moan, she arched beneath him, and Alex fought the temptation to sink his cock into her soft folds. They had all night for pleasure, and he intended to savor every minute.

His lips seared a path down her neck. "Mmm… Here?"

Aine wrapped her arms around his neck. "Nae."

He cupped her warm breast and gazed lovingly into eyes he adored. "Or here?"

"Not there." Her voice husky with desire spurred him onward.

His hand slid over her thigh to her curls. "Would ye like me to taste your sweet honey?"

She shook her head. "Later." Her tongue darted out along her bottom lip, teasing him further.

Taking his thumb, he traced a path over her mouth. "Here?"

Her smile came slowly. "Aye, *my warrior*. Kiss

me."

On a growl, Alex covered her mouth hungrily, devouring the softness of her lips, and giving his Aine all the love in his heart.

Note from the Author...

I hope you've enjoyed *Wishes Under a Highland Star*. This story wraps up the last son of Clan MacFhearguis. In writing Alex and Aine's story, I found a part of my love story woven into theirs. The stars did collide when I first set my sight on the man who would later become my husband. So yes, I do believe in love at first sight. My knight, though tarnished, was older, brooding, and very much like Alex. But we fell passionately in love, and the rest is history.

To research Alex MacFhearguis, I had to travel back in time to when he first stepped through a story, specifically, *Dragon Knight's Sword*. With each book in the *Order of the Dragon Knights* series, I found a stern, quiet, yet complex character. He hid his angst well at being thrust into the role of leader to the MacFhearguis clan. In addition, the loss of his younger brother, Adam, haunted him. When this chieftain encountered a half-Fae lass, he believed himself not worthy of her. However, Aine Fraser proved him wrong each and every moment. She accepted and loved all of the man—scars and flaws.

What's next on the horizon? I'm returning to the Wolves of Clan Sutherland! This man is known for his exceptional battles fought at sea. In his search to seek the ultimate treasure for Scotland—a prize valued by both Norse Gods and Kings—Steinar MacDougall must surrender what he treasures the most.

Until then, may your dreams be filled with Irish charm, Highland mists, and the Wolves of Clan Sutherland!

Psst, don't forget to make a wish under a star. You never know who might appear on a starry night.

A word about the author...

Award-winning Celtic paranormal and fantasy romance author, Mary Morgan, resides in Northern California, with her own knight in shining armor. However, during her travels to Scotland, England, and Ireland, she left a part of her soul in one of these countries and vows to return.

Mary's passion for books started at an early age along with an overactive imagination. Inspired by her love for history and ancient Celtic and Norse mythology, her tales are filled with powerful warriors, brave women, magic, and romance. Now, the worlds she created in her mind are coming to life within her stories.

If you enjoy history, tortured heroes, and a wee bit of magic, then time-travel within the pages of her books.

Visit Mary's website where you'll find links to all of her books, blog, and pictures of her travels.

http://www.marymorganauthor.com